He cleared the last hill that led down to his cabin when he heard a screech. It was Giana. Something was wrong, she was frightened. Pouring on the speed, he darted around trees in his path. He should shift. The thought was replaced with panic, but if the threat was serious, what was he going to do buck ass naked? There was no choice, he had to stay in this form, whether man or beast was the cause of her fear, he could deal with them in this form, at least until he got to his guns.

As he reached the house, he slowed down so he could assess what was happening before running into whatever situation was on the other side of it.

"I am not scared of you," Giana said with a venomous tone. "Just stay away from me and get out of here."

Deacon had to keep a lid on his animal, it wanted to rush in and save their mate. He glanced at the truck, getting there and getting a gun was going to take some fast moves. He heard the door of the porch close. They were inside his home.

ANIMAL SENSES
1 *Heart*
2 *Scent*
3 *Passion*
4 *Courage*
5 *Solace*
6 *Faith*
Coming soon:

7 Spirit
8 Fury
9 Pride
10 Torment

MAGIC SEASONS ROMANCE
1 *Beltane Magic*
2 *Solstice Heat*
3 *Harvest Dreams*
4 *Autumn Dance*
5 *Winter Mist*

Dreams
Three steamy stories that started with a dream

Curses
Two tales of curses.

After the Silence

SINGLE TITLES
Solitary Witchling
Salvation
Café Serenity

Coming soon:
Outcasts

<u>**Writing As: J. Risk**</u>

REALMS BOOKS:

THE ALTEREALM SERIES
1 *The Huntress*
2 *The Seer*
3 *The Empath*
4 *The Witch*
5 *The Chronos*
6 *The Warrior*
7 *The Telepath*
8 *The Healer*
9 *The Kinetic*

THE SOLRELM SERIES
Coming soon:

Concealed

GEMINI LEAGUE
Coming soon

Dark Moon

FAITH

Animal Senses Series Book 6

Jacqueline Paige

Chapter One

She *never* should have stopped back home. Gia cursed at herself, "what possessed you to do that?" She did not have a choice if she wanted more of her belongings. After spending the last week and a half with Amari, she realized this job, the new world that the Clan co-ordinator job showed her that was it for her, she wasn't turning back.

Smirking, she looked around the van. "I guess this is home now." Things had not gone well with her parents, at all. They hadn't told her not to come back, well, not outright, but it had been implied that she either straightened up and worked *with* them and their beliefs of what the daughter of an Alpha was or not being part of the family.

Closing the tote, she assessed if she'd done everything Amari had suggested. All personal 'shit' in a small tote, with a lock, backpack with a change of clothes, hygiene items, and your run pack. All the rest of the gear was secured under the two bench seats that ran along the sides of the van. Shutting the door, she turned around and looked down the road. Freedom. This was new and something she'd wanted for most of her twenty-four years of life.

Riding with Amari Hughes had both been educational and

enlightening. She was also the daughter of an Alpha, they'd connected on so many levels, and Gia was still shocked by it. Her entire life she'd thought she was alone, and it was just her that wasn't all gaga with being part of the Alpha family, Amari set that straight right off.

"Okay," she patted the side of the van and then went and got in the driver's seat. "I'm going to nail this first assignment and show them all that this is what I am meant to do." Pulling out of the parking lot, she tapped the GPS to double-check her own route. She had a day of driving ahead of her before she reached this 'safe house' many of them were going to be at. The details of what they were all doing were sketchy, but according to Amari that was for her own safety. Gia didn't care about the details right now. She was just happy to be on the road and driving in the opposite direction of her family.

Her phone lit up and started playing circus music. Her favorite of her four brothers. She grinned and answered the phone. "Hey, bro."

"Sister, my heart." Walker chuckled.

She glanced at the time on the radio's clock. "I expected you to call a few hours ago."

"I had to get out of the house before I could call, you know that." She heard a door close and knew he was probably hiding in his office at the clan's community building. "I can't believe you did that."

"You heard?"

Walker snorted, "the whole clan probably heard."

She blew out a breath, "I just couldn't…"

"I know, I know. I'm not saying you were wrong, just— you've got balls, Gia, to go toe to toe with Dad like that."

Gia searched inside to see if she felt bad for yelling at their father, when she couldn't find a trace of remorse, she shrugged. "I have no purpose there. None. Why can't he see that?"

"I know, babes, Mom does too, but she'd never speak out against him, you know that." There was a quiet pause, "you will come back sometimes though, right?"

"I don't know, Walker, I don't know right now. The Co-ord team doesn't get a lot of downtime lately…"

"Which is fucking amazing if you ask me, that the Alliance is finally closing in on that Tomas dick and getting our kind out of there."

Gia nodded, "and I get to be a part of it. I have purpose and I am going to nail this job and make Dad see."

"Well, don't hold your breath there. Shit, I better go, Vance and Nash are coming this way and they have that look."

"What look?"

"Oh, the one that says, what-the-hell-did-our-sister-do-this-time, look."

She grinned, "good luck with that. Tell them I'm on my way to meet a team on the other side of the border."

"Shh, no discussing things over open lines, Dad drilled that into all of us before you made him go red in the face."

"I know. Love you bro."

"Be careful, babes."

The line clicked and then was silent. She blew out a breath, feeling bad that Walker was going to have to go face to face with two of their brothers. Brothers. She had more than enough of those. Gia was the youngest and only female of five children. Worse than that, she was a surprise and born later than the 'planned' Alpha family. She always figured it couldn't have been too much of a surprise, as shifters knew when they could or couldn't conceive. It made her feel better most times, that her mother had wanted her. It also proved her father was clueless about some things. So her birth was a win-win. She felt like a heel though, that she couldn't be the perfect only daughter to an Alpha wife.

Picturing Walker and his wordiness all up in Nash and Vance's faces made her grin. Nash was the oldest sibling and very much fit the Alpha's expectations of the son to take over, Vance was the third son and almost a carbon copy of him. They both had perfect little petite, complacent mates, and she was sure would soon have perfectly behaved Alpha family children. "You've got this, bro." Walker was the only brother she got along with, the only one that silently backed her up. He would never say so in front of their father, but they'd spent many hours hidden somewhere talking about everything. His support, regardless of whether it was masked most of the time, meant everything to her.

Gia pictured her second oldest brother's reaction if he'd been at the house. Nox wouldn't have quietly stood on the sidelines. He never did. He wasn't training for Alpha leadership, but he was a big *macho man* on the incursion team. Gia had every confidence that he was good at his job, he was great with hand-to-hand and weapons, it was his personality that she found so flawed she would leave the room anytime he visited. She didn't know the first thing about what he did. She imagined his whole team was comprised of large, opinionated he-man types though.

Life with four older brothers was not something she would wish on anyone. Your every waking moment, every decision, and every step you took was overridden by their opinion of what they thought you *should* be doing.

Her shoulders tensed, just thinking about her brothers did that to her. Except for Walker, she really did adore him. If it hadn't been for him setting her up for secret self-defense training, she would have died a slow and boring death as she grinned and bowed her head as the Alpha's 'showpiece' daughter. Of course, she could never tell anyone else in her family he'd done that, or he'd be an outcast too. She'd excelled at the training and kept going with as much as she could come up with excuses as to what she told others she was doing.

Her phone lit up with a text message, she tapped it to read. It was from her brother Nox, *Keep your head on a swivel.*

She looked back at the road, what did that even mean? With her teeth clenched in a huge fake smile, she tapped it and sent him back a thumb's up emoji.

"Head on a swivel." She snorted, "what am I, an owl?" Picking up her worn baseball cap off the dash, she jammed it on her head. If she'd been born a male, none of this would have been a problem. Turning up the radio, she settled back and focused on the road.

~

Gia was impressed with how far she'd gotten so far. Traffic had been good, but then again, she was doing what Amari suggested and always taking the less obvious route. Amari had told her in confidence what was going on inside the Alliance and Gia had been shocked by it. What kind of shifter would rat out their own kind to someone like Aiden Tomas or any of his associates? It had cemented things in her mind, she was going to do this job and help as many as she could.

Her phone lit up and she was startled to see it was Jesse, the leader of the co-ord team. Muting the music, she hit speaker on the phone. "Jesse, hi."

"Gia, how are you doing?"

"I'm making good time. I crossed the," she stopped, not sure what she should or shouldn't say over the phone.

"All the team phones are secure." He said quietly.

"Okay, uh, I crossed the border about twenty minutes ago. The location Amari said she used."

"Good. Several of ours work at that location."

She pushed her hat up, a little surprised by that. She was learning so much about the Alliance, things she could never have dreamed.

"Listen, I wanted to give you a heads up, your father called the Alliance."

Gia's heart stuttered. Was this where he told her she was off the team and being sent back home? "Oh."

"Too bad the king was busy, and the call was sent to his son, Devin."

She watched the road, afraid to look at the phone. "I'm sorry if my dad…"

"Devin told him that you were an integral part of the co-ord team." He sounded like he was grinning.

"Oh." She didn't know what else to say.

"What was he going to do, argue with the prince?"

The prince had stood up for her with her father for her to stay on the team? "I don't know what to say."

"Hey, you're now one of us and the king is behind my decision to have you on the team, so Alpha or not, your father is just going to have to accept that."

"Thank you. Uh, I don't even know if I'm allowed to go home again."

"You're going to be on the road a lot for the next while, so we'll deal with that later, okay?"

She nodded, feeling weepy and grateful. "Yes."

"The reason I called is, a decision was just made to change things up a bit, after some recent events, it's for everyone's safety."

She sat straighter, "Okay."

"From now on when you're transporting or heading into unknown clan territory a member of the incursion team will be traveling with you."

"Oh." Her heart felt like it was running out of steam as it slowed in her chest. "Um, do we get to pick or…"

"It was going to be randomly assigned by who is closest and if any ops are running, why?"

She cleared her throat. "My brother, Nox, is part of that team."

Jesse sounded like he laughed, "you'd prefer not to have him ride with you?"

"If at all possible, yes." She said quietly, afraid to breathe.

"Okay, I'll tell Zain of your wishes." This time he did chuckle.

"Thank you." The breath she hadn't realized she was holding whooshed out of her lungs.

"When you're closer to Chicago, shoot Zain a text and he'll give you the exact location. We're not sending anything out in advance from now on."

"Okay, I can do that."

"And Gia?"

"Yes?"

"Welcome to the team. I'll see you when you reach the safe house."

She smiled. "Thank you, Jesse."

Gia swatted at the tear rolling down her cheek. Now was not the time to turn all 'sappy female'. Sucking in a deep breath, she blew it out. She had the prince and the King of the Alliance backing her up, that kind of support she could get used to.

Chapter Two

Deacon glanced over to see Nox drop his phone into the cup holder. His expression wasn't good. "Problems?"

Nox shifted in the seat to a more comfortable position. "Sister."

"Ah." He said it as if he understood, but he didn't, not really.

"She let herself be recruited to the clan coordination team." He made a noise of annoyance.

"That's a problem?" Deacon had met many of the members of that team, their job wasn't an easy one.

"Yeah, that's a problem. She's an Alpha's daughter and shouldn't be doing shit like that." He huffed out a breath picked up the coffee cup and gave it a shake to see if there was anything left in it.

Deacon didn't voice it, but he didn't agree. Having a member of an Alpha family visiting other clans seemed like good optics to him—especially with some of the rivaling clans' disagreements they'd seen and been sent to peacefully oversee. "I met a woman on that team, she's Alpha too, Amari…"

"Amari is different and completely capable of looking after herself."

"You don't think your sister is?" He looked back at the road, "capable?"

"Sure, she can track and shit for fun competitions, but this is the real world, man, she has no idea."

Deacon went through half a dozen replies in his head, none of which would have earned him any points, so he settled on saying something to pass the focus to someone else. "Jesse is a straight-up kind of guy; I don't see him allowing someone on the team if he doesn't think they're capable."

He felt Nox's eyes on him but didn't bother looking over.

"Let's hope he knows what he's doing." Nox picked up his phone, "my dad is pissed. According to Nash, the prince backed my sister being on the team." He snorted, "I know you're not from a clan, so you don't get it, but this is causing a lot of rifts in my world right now."

Nox always did that, brought up Deacon's past, like it was the reason for anything that wasn't going the way the man wanted. Truth be told, in his opinion Deacon had worked harder and proven himself by going from clan less to working for the king. Deacon pulled his cap down further to shade his eyes, "well, if Jesse and the prince say she's golden, then I guess she is." He glanced at him to be met with an unamused look, "have a little faith—man."

Nox made another sound of annoyance and then turned and looked out the window, "yeah whatever."

Deacon reached into the pocket of his vest and pulled out a new mint-flavored toothpick. Clamping it between his teeth, he focused on the road. They'd crossed the border and since the back tires had moved over that invisible line, his guts were in knots. He hated this side of the border. There was nothing but bad memories of violence and hunger pains over here for him. He rolled his head from one side to the other, trying to loosen the tension in his neck. He couldn't afford to get bogged down with that shit right now. Things were really heating up with his team and the whole Alliance, there was no time for emotional history. Deacon was primed and ready to lay a beat down on all that was a part of Aiden Tomas' world.

He glanced at Nox again to see he was glaring out the window. Deacon didn't dare say he knew who his sister was, that would end about as well as a nuclear bomb going off. He'd met the petite, sexy little fireball, Giana Marin at a gathering of the clans almost five years ago. She'd taken his breath away and made his animal want to howl at the sky. She was his mate, and he was so unworthy of a female like her. He'd run like a coward from the gathering and called Calum Dante as he drove his rusted-out, duct-taped truck off the property. Calum had helped to steer him in the right direction, and he hadn't looked back since then.

He'd spent four years proving to himself and any doubters that he was a worthy male and a force to be reckoned with. If it weren't for Calum, Deacon probably would have died in that backwoods shack a long time ago. Calum had found his sick, half-starved, pathetic ass and brought him back with him. That man was the reason Deacon did what he did now, help others. Not everyone had the strength and means to control their life's direction. Deacon liked to believe he was part of balancing the scales for those in need.

It had taken him two years to prove his allegiance to the Alliance and king and then another two of busting his hump to get on the Incursion team and prove his worth there and nothing was going to make him turn away from it now. Not some Alpha family brother, that was for sure.

Deacon hadn't seen Giana in all that time, but in the back of his mind, she was always there. She was the driving force and reason he changed his body, his health, his entire being, on the chance that if he ever had the balls to face her again, they would be on more equal ground. Of course, there was a good chance he'd swallow his own tongue and asphyxiate on it if he did see her again, but that was up to fate and he had all the faith in the world that what was meant to be, would be.

His phone ringing had him jerk as if someone had poked him. It was his boss, he hit it and put it on speaker, then looked over to see Nox was aware of who it was too. "Boss?"

"Deacon, you're with Nox, right?"

"I'm right here." Nox was sitting upright in the seat now like she could see he was at attention or something.

"Good, one less call—because I have time to play fucking secretary here."

They both smirked at her tone, Wynter Carr was not an a-typical female in any way at all. She was blunt, and rude and Deacon was pretty sure she wasn't even aware that she was a female most times.

"I just got a call from Devin Addison. From now on when the co-ord team is transporting or going into unknown situations, one of us ride shotgun."

Nox nodded his head. He was such a yes-man, suck-up sometimes it turned Deacon's stomach.

Deacon looked back at the road, "did something happen to cause this change?"

Wynter made a sound like she wanted to spit, "yeah, someone tranq'd Jesse and had plans to take off with his mate," she laughed that deep almost manly laugh of hers, "haven't met her, but I plan to, she put a bullet right in one of their hearts from fifty feet away."

That got Nox's attention.

"Everyone all right?" Deacon was smirking, but it was more from his passenger's reaction than from the fact that a woman made an awesome shot.

"They're fine. Keeping her location on the hush from now on though."

Deacon nodded. "All right. There's a lot of *hush* happening now."

"I don't know how those sadistic bastards are finding ours, but I plan to take the unkind end of my rifle and jam it right up their…" there were voices in the background for a moment. "Zain, from the Alliance offices, will be sending you boys locations and shit to assist the co-ord team from now on. Solid?"

"Yeah, Boss." Nox answered fast.

"Got it." Deacon looked at the road marker they'd just passed, "we should reach our destination in the next two hours."

They could hear her cursing someone out in the background, "that shit has been back burner'd, I'm *told*, the new destination will be sent to you shortly." She cleared her throat, "keep it tight, I'll be talking to you both tonight sometime."

"Will do." Deacon reached forward and hung up before Nox could say something else that could only be labeled 'kiss ass'.

"Damn this is getting intense." Nox turned around grabbed the cooler and dragged it closer to the seats.

"Jesse must have one hell of a mate." Deacon grinned.

"Tranq darts, what's with that shit?" Nox mumbled.

Deacon shifted his hat back on his head and rubbed his hand over his forehead. "It's new." He glanced at him, "and means we're going to have to have our heads on a swivel all the time now."

Nox nodded, "yeah, just what we need." He looked back out the window.

Deacon clamped his teeth down on the toothpick. If they were going to be helping members of the co-ord team, at some point he was bound to run into Giana. His heart felt like it was doing the obstacle course right now. He wanted to see her more than his next breath, but *that* was also the reason he'd avoided seeking her out all this time. Shit was getting intense all right and he didn't know if he was going to come out the other end of it unscathed.

Chapter Three

Gia stared at the dash as she turned the key. Nothing was happening. At all. She closed her eyes, "great. I broke it on my first solo trip." She debated for about three seconds of opening the hood and looking, but she knew as much about vehicles as she did brain surgery. Blowing out a breath, she picked up her phone and brought up Zain's number. She hit the call button before she could change her mind.

"Giana?"

"Gia," she corrected. "The van died."

"What do you mean died?"

She shook her head and got out. "I mean I was driving along and then it just turned off and now nothing."

"That's impossible. It was just at the shop for a complete car spa day, it should be working, it should be purring like a damn cat."

"Maybe it didn't like the spa." She smirked.

"Shit. Hang on, I'm going to bring up your location on the tracking app," she could hear him typing, "hang on a sec, Jesse is on the other line."

"I'm not going anywhere." She turned in a circle and looked around. There was absolutely nothing here. Except for fields, long grass, and the odd tree. That was it. To make the insult of screwing up her first solo trip worse, she had to pee and could be stuck here for a while.

"Gia, help has been called, uh, I guess just sit tight until they get there."

"Okay, Zain," she grinned, "tell them to bring a burger too, I'm starving."

"Ha, I'll get right on that." There were voices in the background, "I gotta go. Let me know when they're there."

"Okay, thank you." Reaching in the van, she grabbed her run pack and then grabbed the keys and jammed them in her pocket. Locking the door, she closed it, then debated which direction she was going to find a shrub or something.

Gia wandered across the field toward the trees. Okay, so some parts of her were girly, she liked the color the leaves turned in the fall. She just wanted to take a few up-close pictures of them for her own collection.

Her phone ringing startled her. She answered it without looking at the caller. "Hello?"

"Gia."

It was Jesse. "I'm sorry…"

He snorted, "the van dying isn't your fault. I have no idea why it would, I'm just thankful it did it now and not two days from now."

She hadn't thought of that. If she'd been transporting rescues, it could have endangered all of them.

"Someone is going to be getting an earful from Devin, so you can be sure it will never happen again."

"Okay." She turned back to see a car pulling up behind the van. Two big men got out of it. She grinned, "hey your guys made great time getting here. They're already here."

"What? Gia, our guys have *just* left the shop." He barked into the phone.

Gia dropped to her knees and crouched down so she wasn't visible.

"Gia?"

"I'm hiding in the grass." She whispered.

"Tell me what you see." She could hear other voices in the background now.

"Uh," she tried to see without making her location known, "just a second," taking off the dark cap, she hoped her red hair blended better with the fall foliage and moved along on her elbows and toes toward the trees she'd originally been heading to. When she reached them, she dragged her body over the damp ground until she could use a tree to hide her. Looking around it, she kept low so no one could notice her, "okay, I'm hidden now," she whispered, "there's two of them, really big men," she watched the one walk along the side of the van and look in the driver's window, the other one was standing out front of the van looking in the field on that side of the road. He had a handgun in his hand, "they have guns." She said breathlessly.

"Listen to me," Jesse's voice was calm and steady, "Webb and I aren't that far from you, and a couple of other teams are nearby, we're coming to you as soon as I hang up."

"Okay."

"You find somewhere to hole up and stay there, we'll find you."

Gia looked around in the trees, this bush area wasn't very big, it was sparse too, no way she could run through it and not be seen. Peeking out around the tree again, she saw that the other man was looking across the road now in her direction. "I'm going to shift." She said quickly, "I can get further. I'm on the opposite side of the road to the van." She added in case they'd need a direction to start.

"Keep your phone on you, we have a tracker on the number."

She nodded, as she leaned down and took off her boots. Dammit, she couldn't load her pack with her clothes, she needed to be light and fast. "I'm not taking my clothes, just my phone in my pack." She opened the pack and took out the snacks and water bottle.

"Stay safe, we'll be there soon."

She nodded and didn't have a chance to say any more before the line went quiet. Looking at the phone, she double-checked to make sure he'd hung up. She was alone. She nodded to herself as she stuffed the phone in her pack and put it over her head. She tightened the strap a bit, so it wouldn't get snagged on anything.

Checking once more, her heart felt like it was in her throat when she saw both men standing there now looking in the same direction she was, finding somewhere to stay out of sight may prove difficult. Sliding down, she prayed the tree and grass hid her completely. Pulling off her hoodie, then her t-shirt and leggings, she rolled them into a ball. She'd just bought that hoodie and wasn't impressed she was leaving it behind. As a fox shifter though, she wasn't large, so she couldn't cart a wardrobe around with her as big clans could.

Checking that the pack was zipped up, she blew out a breath and shifted. She'd have to stay low until she put a few more trees between them and her. Looking one last time at her clothes, she turned and took off into the trees, zigzagging between them, making herself hard to track.

She scented around her, and didn't pick up any nearby wildlife, that made it easier, she didn't need any confrontations to add to her not-great day. It took a lot of concentration to keep going and not turn around and look back to see what those men were doing. They had guns and hers was under the seat of the van, so it was a no-brainer that running was the best option this time. She wasn't sure if she could shoot a living thing, but now wasn't the time to find out either.

She went flying past a rotting log and then put on the brakes and slid over the ground. Going back, she scented the log, and the area around it, there were no markings of a wild creature that she could detect. Moving closer, she checked under the log to see an old burrow was there. That year of running in bushes to escape her family had done some good, she knew instinctively where the best locations were for burrows and dens.

Scanning behind her, she froze, becoming statuesque, and

moved only her eyes to see if she had anyone coming up on her. She didn't see anything, she inhaled slowly, and the scent of rank cologne came to her. No shifter, with a brain, wore anything perfumed. They weren't just on the wrong side of right; they were lacking normal shifter values and common sense too.

Putting her belly to the ground, she moved so her head was in the opening of the burrow and inhaled slowly, she couldn't pick up anything that told her this was some creatures' home. That was a bonus, the last thing she needed was to pull a Goldilocks and be in someone else's home when they came back.

She hated every second of having to do this, but there was no way those two behemoths were intelligent enough to look in a barely visible hole in the ground. Baring her teeth at the thought of doing something like this, she jumped over the log and then relieved herself on the brown grass. *Snort that*, she thought as she jumped back over it and crouched down to creep into the burrow.

Her fox was one of the smaller animals in their world, but still bigger than the real ones. There was a moment of feeling stuck as she squeezed her larger body down the tunnel, hopefully, it was a normal den dugout after this, or she was going to be in a bigger mess than she already was.

Focusing on her breathing, she kept herself calm as she reached the bottom and then turned awkwardly so she was facing out again. The inner part had a faint scent of a real fox, a long-ago abandoned den. She didn't let herself think of what had caused them to move away and not return, although, with no wildlife scents in the area, that could have been it—no prey to hunt.

Shuffling, keeping her body scrunched up, she moved back up toward the entrance, so she could at least hear if they were close to her location or not. When she stopped, she had a second of panic feeling like she was buried alive. What if they breezed right by here and she wasn't found? *Get it together. This is what you want.* Closing her eyes, trying to slow her breathing. The slower she managed the less she felt like the soil pushing against her. *Could be worse, you could be sitting at a luncheon with your mother and all the female mates in the clan discussing new gardens for next year.* Yeah, as pep talks went, that did the trick. Good thing she had some girly bits in her and was drawn to those pretty leaves was her next thought, or she would have been standing beside the van when they pulled up.

She couldn't hear any movement at all, which made her start to wonder if she'd hear Jesse when they got her to retrieve her. She shifted, so she could feel her pack, assuring herself that she still had it. Had she silenced the ringer? She had no idea. He said they could track it—did that work with her hiding in a burrow under the earth? *Be a good tracker, Jesse.*

Chapter Four

Deacon pulled up behind the other van as Jesse got out of it. There was another male with him that he didn't know, but he was huge, and just looking at him, made Deacon think of a bear. He tossed the chewed toothpick out the window.

Nox jumped out and slammed the door, then rushed over to Jesse.

Taking a second, Deacon communicated with his animal, assuring him that their mate was fine, and they would find her. Turning his hat around backward, he got out and headed over to the other men.

He reached the van in time to see the expression on Nox's face as Jesse told him to stay with the vehicles in case the others came back. Normally he'd have volunteered to do it, but Giana was out there somewhere and there was no way he'd be able to stand idly by.

Deacon turned from the others and inhaled slowly. Even after the years that had passed, he'd know that scent anywhere. He could still taste it in his dreams. She'd crossed the road and gone toward those trees. Without a word, he started down through the ditch.

He may have been invisible from her life, but he'd kept tabs on what she'd been doing. She was smart, he already knew that. The tracking events at the gatherings weren't easy routes and she'd won many of them. He felt like a creeper, staying out of scent range with binoculars watching her more times than he cared to count. He'd had to do it though to assure his animal and his mind that their mate was fine over the years.

Her scent led to the thinned-out trees, and he could almost picture her fox darting through them, creating a hard-to-follow trail, he kept his head up and followed the sweet bouquet that smelled of jasmine, floral but musky at the same time. Her, it was all her. He spotted her clothes and went over. Pausing, he picked them up and rolled them into a ball. Jesse came up beside him. He bent down and picked up the boots.

"The stench of cologne was by the van," Jesse said in a low tone, "but I haven't picked it up this way."

Deacon shook his head, "they didn't follow her."

"They probably figured we'd picked her up and left the van for the shop to retrieve."

Deacon nodded, not wanting to have a long-drawn-out conversation. He jerked his chin, "she went this way."

Jesse motioned to the other man to head through the trees.

With her clothes balled up in his off-hand, he kept his other hovering close to the sidearm strapped to his thigh. He had to keep his breathing level and his animal on lockdown for fear that if he saw anything move that wasn't rusty orange colored, he might make it a target out of the rage that was trying to consume him. It had been a struggle since Jesse had called and said who it was that was in trouble.

Someone had gone after his mate. Somehow, they'd followed her and tracked her. Her van dying on the side of the road couldn't be a coincidence, there was no way. He'd seen the service list for all Alliance vehicles, there was no way it would be run down to the point it just quit. He knew a little about vehicles, he could replace parts, but wasn't going to be able to prove that theory. It wasn't even a guess, his gut told him they were behind her being stranded out here, alone and that somehow, they'd followed her.

He stopped and inhaled again, moving just his eyes through the quiet space. She'd bounced around in the trees like it was a maze, making the trail harder to find. His mouth moved into a lopsided grin, his mate was a wily one, that was for sure.

Inside him, his animal was pacing, agitated, hard to keep reigned in. He paused again and emitted a low growl, a vocal order to get it together or they'd be in a whole different bad situation. The man with Jesse crouched down and looked around slowly. Deacon gave him a quick shake of his head, "just a warning." He said mostly under his breath but knew the shifter would hear him from that distance.

Deacon pointed into the trees telling both other men the direction she went. The warning was for his own animal, the last thing he needed was for her to see what he was. What had Maxton called him before he'd left the group he'd grown up with? Oh yeah, an abomination. His creature was the only reason he'd been able to stay away from her all this time, he knew that was never going to be allowed to happen.

With long strides he walked in a straight line, he didn't need to duck around trees and other obstacles. He paused and looked at a rotting tree, with long growth all around it. His animal was suddenly in hunt mode, reminding him of their life before. The best place to find a meal was in a location like that.

He swept his arm toward the spot and didn't bother to look and see if Jesse and that other male moved in that direction. He could smell her, stronger than ever. Shaking off a moment of want, he kept going toward it. The large male walked around to the other side of a dead tree and looked in that direction.

Deacon looked to see Jesse was watching him and not looking around. He motioned to the flattened grass leading under the log. Jesse raised an eyebrow but went over carefully, when he grinned, Deacon knew his instincts had been right and she was hiding in some other creatures' home.

Jesse squatted down, "Gia." He said loud enough that his voice would carry beneath the layers of earth. "It's Jesse." He straightened and backed up as her copper-colored head appeared from between the grasses. Backing up, he set her boots down and glanced over at the other man.

The big guy shrugged and started back to this side, "and that is why I'm not a tracker." He shrugged, "I'll go call the rest of the team and tell them we have her."

Jesse nodded, "find out where the hell that tow truck is too, Webb."

Webb nodded but made no further comment as he walked silently back toward the road. His stealthy movement momentarily surprised Deacon, for a big man he was light on his feet.

Turning back, Deacon looked down at Gia as she shook the dirt from her coat. A brief inclination to bend down and hug her to him crossed his mind. He sobered, knowing that all it would get him was her teeth sunk into his body. His creature stirred; he'd be okay with her biting him.

Moving as close as he dared, he tossed her clothes to land in front of her. He couldn't have spoken if he'd wanted to as her grey eyes looked up at him and perused him slowly.

"We'll, uh, be over here while you shift back and get dressed." Jesse motioned a few feet away.

Deacon had to force his legs to move in that direction, to turn his back to her. He rested his hand on the gun, as his eyes tracked over the long grass and weeds, watching for any movement of any kind. Looking over at the van, he watched Nox pace back and forth beside it. He wasn't even paying attention to the road, watching for other vehicles. Deacon wasn't a rat, but he still lifted his hand and motioned to the prancing brother Jesse had left beside the vehicle.

Jesse sighed, "he's her brother and from what I gathered earlier she'd prefer not to be face to face with him."

"You are right."

Both men turned to Gia. She was pulling on her hoodie.

"He'd only tell me everything I did wrong and how I shouldn't be here." She said as she brushed some leaves from her leggings.

Jesse shook his head, "you did everything right." He motioned to Deacon, "if Deacon wasn't here, we would have walked right by where you were."

Gia peered at him, her eyes moving over him like she was trying to decipher him for a moment. "Thank you." She blew out a breath, and tucked her hair up under the hat, "now if you'll excuse me, I need to go tell Nox to stuff his idea of what I should be doing."

Deacon could only stand there and watch her stomp in the direction of the vehicles and her anxious brother.

Jesse glanced at him, "I'm not sure if I should interfere or stand back and watch Nox get his ass handed to him." He smirked.

Deacon could only nod, he was consumed with the scent of her that had filled every fiber of his body as she'd walked by him.

Jesse started walking back, he pulled out his phone and looked at it. As he walked, he typed something into it quickly.

Lurching as if he'd just broken his cemented feet free, Deacon went after him, "Jesse, I don't think this was a fluke."

Jesse stopped and waited for him to catch up. "What do you mean?"

Rubbing a hand over his beard, he regretted it immediately, it had been the hand that carried her clothes and now he could taste her. Her scent was going to linger in his beard for hours now. "Uh, the van," he spurred his brain to function, "it quitting—I think it was on purpose."

Jesse looked at the van and then back to him, "you think it was deliberate?"

He nodded, "think about it, how often are they serviced?" He shrugged, "more than once mine's been called in for a once over when it wasn't required."

Jesse looked at the vehicle as they continued to walk. "I don't know how they would do that." He waved a hand toward it, "she would have known if she was being followed, there isn't exactly a lot of traffic here."

They walked through the ditch and went over to it. He tried to ignore the immovable stance of Nox standing there with his arms over his chest as Giana waved her hand around inches from his face. Dragging his attention back to the incapacitated vehicle, he stared at the back of it. "Paint cans." He said under his breath.

"What?" Jesse turned around and looked at him.

"Uh, just remembering something." It was true, the group he'd landed in with when he'd first left the wanderers had been up to some underhanded things. When they found a vehicle, they wanted to track, they'd secure a punctured can under it to leave a trail. "I think it's being tracked somehow."

"Son of a bitch." Jesse said under his breath, "they found me," he looked back to Deacon, "when I had my mate with me and went after us."

Deacon nodded, "Wynter told us."

"I've been going over that in my head a hundred times, trying to figure out how—I never do anything predictable." He turned and stared at the van he and Webb had gotten out of. "Shit." He pulled his phone back out. He pointed to Giana's van, "give her a hand getting all her gear out of that one and into mine."

Deacon nodded and went over to the van. She had the driver's door open now and was mumbling under her breath to herself.

Turning his hat back to the front, so the bill of it would shadow his face, he opened the back door. "Jesse says to move everything to his van." He told her when she looked at him from the front of it.

"Yeah, okay." She blew out a breath, her forehead was puckered, and he could feel the tension pouring off her.

"You did great," he told her, hoping to wipe that expression off her face. "The only reason I didn't blow right by that log was that I spent a lot of time in the bush monitoring wildlife when I was younger."

Her face lit up as if he'd just told her she won the lottery. "Thank you." She looked through the window at her brother who was glaring at her from where he stood. "*Some* people think I'm a half-wit without a brain in my head."

Deacon lifted one shoulder in a small shrug, "some people should keep their opinion to themself."

A slamming door had him jolt and spin around. Jesse walked around to the front of his van and popped the hood on it. He stood there looking in it now. "Think about it, Devin, how else did they know when I'd hit that stretch of road?" He stared at the motor like the answer was going to jump out at him. Webb went over and looked in it with him, he moved the phone from his mouth and looked at him, "Webb, go look and see if you can see anything obvious done to hers that would cause it to stop running."

Webb gave him a skeptical look and then nodded before walking around to the front of Gia's van.

Gia popped the release lever for the hood and went around the front. "You think something was done to it?"

Webb lifted his big hand and shrugged, "the boss says look, I look." He opened the hood and leaned over it, moving his head to peer down in between things.

"That's," she spun around and looked at her brother and then back to Webb, "How? When?"

Nox, now scowling with a look of focus on his face went over and watched Webb. "Did you stop anywhere along the way?"

Gia's expression soured, "a few times, just to stretch my legs. I wasn't away from it for more than a couple of minutes though."

Deacon grabbed the tote and carried it to Jesse's van, opening the back door, he slid it in. His animal was pissed, to the point that he was having to keep his jaw clenched to focus on keeping him on the inside. His skin was hurting, muscles clenching. Someone went after their mate. Taking a deep breath, he closed his eyes for a second and tried to convey that at this point they both needed Deacon on the outside to keep her safe. The creature didn't like it, but it settled just enough that he could function again.

Opening his eyes, he saw Jesse looking at him, but he made no comment as he started talking again and walk to the other side of the road to stand there.

He went back and grabbed the supplies tucked under the

one bench seat.

"Jesse," Webb growled out, his voice not so light and easy-going now.

Deacon walked around the van to see him under the front of it, his body from the waist up almost wedged underneath.

Jesse came over and squatted down, the phone still to his ear.

Deacon leaned over the side of the motor and looked down at the other man

"This wire," Webb moved around, "it's been cut, not corroded."

"What is it to?" Jesse knelt on the road and leaned down to try and look

"Alternator." Nox said, almost in Deacon's ear as he leaned over and looked in the motor as well.

"Did you hear that?" Jesse got to his feet and nodded to whatever was said on the phone, "this was intentional." Jesse nodded, "let me know." He hung up and glared at the van. "Devin's calling back in a minute with a new plan." Jesse squeezed his eyes shut for a second and then opened them. "We have a lot of vehicles out there right now."

Webb worked his way back out from under the bumper. "So," he got to his feet, "I'm guessing they have a way to track our vehicles."

Nox stood there with his hands on his hips and glanced from one to the other.

Jesse rubbed his hand along his jaw. He turned to Deacon, "how's your fund pouch?"

Deacon shrugged, "fine, we haven't used it since the last op."

Jesse nodded slowly, then rolled his shoulders, "we're going to have to ditch the vans and get new rides."

Gia had been busying herself moving things to the other vehicle up to this point, she came over and stood too close to Deacon, he could taste her scent again, "you think they're somehow tracking the vans?" She looked from Jesse to Nox, "all of them?"

Deacon stepped back and looked up and down the road, just to put more distance between them.

"We can't take the chance until we have them all checked," Jesse frowned, "by someone other than the shop we use."

"Isn't the shop run by our kind?" Deacon's brows drew together, not from the conversation, but because he wanted to lean over and lick Giana's exposed throat. He had to get away from her.

Jesse nodded, "most of them, yeah." His tone was low. Blowing out a breath he put his hands on his hips and shook his head slowly, "I don't trust the safe house now either." He swore venomously and lifted his phone again. "I have to get a hold of Calum before they reach it." He stomped to the other side of the road.

Webb cleared his throat, then slammed the hood down, "his mate is with them." He said quietly.

Deacon stomped to the back of his own van and stood there. Every muscle in his body was tight, uncomfortably so. *Shit.* He was going to have to make sure he was assigned to the team that Giana was working with. If someone was after his mate, they'd have to survive him before ever touching her—and their odds of surviving that were less than zero with the way he was feeling right now.

Chapter Five

Gia sat in the open door of the van with her knees drawn up with her feet on the bumper. This was not turning out to be the day she had envisioned at all. She felt a slight bit better, that the van dying hadn't been her fault, but then the realization that it had been messed with sunk in.

Amari hadn't been joking when she said as a female every minute on the road was a risk. She'd known others that had gone missing and heard stories, but to live it was something completely different. She chewed on the inside of her cheek as she watched the four men standing there talking. That was like a symbol of her life right there, four large males talking, not including her. Not that she had anything to add, what did she know about planning and organizing something like this? Nothing. She couldn't offer ideas because her whole life had kept her sheltered from what was going on. Aside from lurking and listening in on conversations, she wasn't part of that.

Jesse was beyond agitated right now and she didn't blame him, his mate could have walked into a trap, or that's what she heard him say to someone on the other end of the phone. They didn't know if the safe house all of them were supposed to be going to was safe now. So here they waited until new plans were formed.

She watched her brother nod like his opinion was necessary. Of course, he would, he wielded his privileged status like a neon sign. The big guy, Webb, stood off to the side, listening to what was being said, but offered no opinions. She liked him, he exuded calmness, if not a little too cavalier emotion.

The big man, Deacon, she knew him. It had taken a moment to realize, but once she saw those steel-blue eyes— they were the kind of eyes you never forgot. Looking at him now, she couldn't believe how he'd changed. They'd met once at a gathering she was competing at and then he'd been this scrawny jerk with a rude mouth. Now, from looking at him, she would say he'd spent the last few years adding muscle to his muscle and that muscle in turn had sculpted even more bulges under his clothes. He'd found her though and for that she was thankful. She hadn't considered that her decoy trail would confuse the people sent to rescue her.

As if he knew she was thinking about him, he turned and looked right at her. Despite the bill of his ball cap shadowing his eyes, she could still feel his intense stare. They were focused and hard, which made his kind words seem strange earlier.

So far, he hadn't offered his thoughts on this predicament, he spent more time watching the road, checking for cars. His hand never strayed far from the gun strapped to his leg. Next to her brother, who had his vest undone and arms crossed, he looked like a super-soldier and not just one of the guys.

Jesse's phone ringing brought an abrupt halt to all conversation. Nox and Webb watched him as he talked, he seemed calmer now. Deacon turned his back to them and looked down the road again, he rolled his big shoulders as if the tension of the world was resting on them. He was good at his job, that much she knew already.

Sliding until her feet touched the ground, she stood up and adjusted her hat, so the sun wouldn't touch her face. She wanted to be that good at her job, she decided. Focused and not distracted by outside elements and events.

Jesse tucked his phone into his pocket. "Truck will be here

in ten." He turned to Nox, "you're to stay with the van and ride with them back to the location," he looked at the van, then back to Nox, "so no one can mess with it until we find out what's been done to it."

Nox glanced at her, and she could see he wasn't happy with not being able to stick with her and nag at her some more about why she should be at home.

"Deacon, you follow in your van, once you get there, leave it and load up into a rental that will be waiting, Zain will give you the new location where we're meeting." Jesse glanced at his phone, "it's more remote than we'd hoped, which will mean more travel time, but it's not on any lists."

Deacon nodded, then looked down the road again.

"Webb, Gia, you're with me. We're going to a second location and picking up two new vehicles." Jesse shook his head, "this is a pain in the ass, but we can't take a chance until the Alliance vehicles have all been checked."

Gia nodded. "Is everything all right with your mate?"

Jesse looked surprised she'd asked, "yeah, Calum rarely uses Alliance vehicles, and no one would mess with his car."

She smiled. "That's good." She knew Calum and was inclined to agree, that no one would ever touch his car and survive it. "How many of us are going to be at this house?"

Jesse raised his eyebrows and blew out a breath, "too many, which is why we're trying to find a second one right now."

"Some of us could crash outside," Deacon offered.

Gia had to hide the smirk Nox's reaction caused. The idea of sleeping outside looked like he'd just been given a death sentence.

Jesse cleared his throat, "if it were summer, I'd agree, but it's getting a little cool for that." He motioned to the vans. "Let's get going. I want to get to the house before Blair does—he's going to be on edge and impatient."

Gia looked from him to Webb, who nodded. She didn't know what was going on. Who was Blair and why was he going to be impatient? Closing the door, she took out her phone and messaged Amari. *Are you going to be where I am?* She had no idea how many this operation was going to involve.

She was getting into the back of Jesse's van when the reply came. *No, I'm still on a quest. Happy and Broody are going to be there. Should be a blast.* So, that was—Asher and Webb? Gia grinned, wondering if the team knew she had nicknames for all of them. Another message came in. *You've got this.*

Closing the door, she replied quickly, *Thanks.*

Jesse glanced back at her and then to the phone in her hand.

"Amari," she said quietly hoping this wasn't breaking any rules. Her phone vibrated again before he could say anything. *Can you believe this shit? It's going to add hours to my trip.* She looked to see him still watching her, "I guess she just found out about the vehicles."

Webb chuckled, "glad I wasn't the one to mess with her timeline. She hates delays."

Jesse smirked and turned back to start the van.

She typed quickly, filtering what she wanted to say, just to be careful. She trusted nothing now after learning about her van. *I know. I think I'm the reason they figured it out.*

I'll call you later when I'm back on track. Stay safe.

You too. Gia turned off the screen and sat holding the phone and looking straight ahead. *You can do this.* She chanted her lifelong mantra in her head. *If you quit, you make your father and brothers right.* She smirked, that always worked when she had doubts.

"You did great today, Gia." Jesse glanced at her in the mirror.

She pasted a cordial smile on her face. "Thanks."

"Your brother wants me to send you somewhere else."

She connected with his reflection in the mirror, holding her breath, biting her tongue so she wouldn't say something rude she'd regret.

"He's not happy I denied his request," Jesse smirked. His phone ringing ended that conversation. Instead of putting it on speaker, he put it to his ear. "I'm fine, babe. How was the trip?" He grinned, "I prefer the jeep too." He sobered, "how's Leah?" He listened and focused on the road. "I'll be there in about an hour, maybe a bit more." He nodded, "me too." He hung up and glanced at Webb, "Cal's car, Cal's driving."

Webb laughed, "you couldn't pay me to wedge my ass in the back of that tiny car."

Chapter Six

Deacon came down the stairs and turned the corner on his heel to go out to the back of the house. The place was huge. Five bedrooms, and an apartment over the three-bay garage. He looked at the two small buildings in the fenced backyard. One looked like a small guest house.

He walked back toward the other small building, giving the two tables in the middle of the yard a look, there were no chairs. Reaching the smaller building, he opened the door and then nodded. *Found the chairs.* Sticking his head in, he spotted a few yard tools hanging up and that was it. Picking up a stack of chairs, he carried them over to the table and set them down beside it.

"Rearranging the yard?"

Deacon jolted and turned to see Calum standing there grinning at him.

"You know you could get yourself shot, sneaking up on me." Deacon grinned, happy to see him.

Calum looked amused, "I wasn't sneaking—you were just lost in that," he waved his hand beside his head, "never-ending monologue you have going on up there." He looked at the shed, "what are you doing?"

Rubbing his fingers over the side of his beard Deacon looked over at the shed. "Figured I'd crash in there." He pointed to the house, "too many walls and bodies in there."

Calum crossed his arms over his chest, "It's going to be cozy."

The sound of a vehicle had them both turn to see Webb pulling one of the new vans up beside the house. He hopped out and then stood there looking at it. Turning, he came toward them. "Think they'll let me keep it? I'm loving the black." He stopped ten feet from them, "toss me your keys, Deacon, we're hiding three of the vehicles on this side of the fence."

Deacon reached in his pocket and pulled them out, he tossed them to Webb.

Catching them, Webb raised both arms in the air. "And the crowd goes wild." Without further antics, he turned and walked back toward the side of the house.

"Is he always so happy?" Deacon turned back to Calum.

He nodded, "afraid so."

A door closed making them both turn to see Jesse standing on the veranda. "Blair's here."

Calum nodded, "come on, things are about to get intense."

Following him, Deacon tried to settle his animal, because being trapped in a house with seventeen other bodies, including their mate wasn't going to be intense enough?

Deacon stood in the kitchen, looking down into the large sunken 'family room'. Too many bodies in one small area. Giana was sitting in a chair by herself. He presumed the woman perched on the arm of the sofa, as close as Jesse was hovering, had to be the man's mate. He was happy with that arrangement; no males were close to his mate.

A man from the same team as Giana came over and stood beside him. He gave Deacon a quick nod, then braced his legs apart, crossing his arms over his chest.

Deacon looked around at the others, he knew a few of them, aside from his team members, Nox and York.

York Meyers was one of the few he could work with

seamlessly; he was quiet and didn't go for the posturing some of his team did. He glanced at Nox as if that proved his point. He sat there, shoulders back like he was trying to make himself seem bigger than he already was.

Out of the seventeen, Deacon recognized seven. That left ten others he'd have to sus out. His gut reflex was to trust no one. He tracked the five males he didn't know. The tall one in the corner was doing some watching of his own. In appearance, he was probably six, seven years younger than he was himself, but his eyes—yeah, Deacon recognized the cold look in them. He'd seen some soul-draining shit in his life.

The other man with the shaggy brown hair that Calum was watching carefully had to be someone special, he'd seen Calum move to position himself between him and the window, three times now.

"Okay, let's get some introductions out of the way so we can figure out the new timeline. How much further is this house?" He looked at Illias, who sat on the stairs.

Illias, Deacon knew. He was a techy guy, although, with the scar that ran from the side of his mouth down his neck, he knew the man hadn't always been a behind-the-scenes tech.

"Twenty minutes," Illias answered.

"Okay, adjust the routes and times to compensate for that."

The woman with the long blonde hair gave the one talking an amused look, "Devin, the introductions."

He stopped and turned to look at her. "Fuck." He whispered, even though all the shifters would hear him. "I'm Devin, this is my lovely mate, Rayne." He smiled at her and then held up his hand. "There will be none of that bowing *shit*, okay? We don't have time for that *stuff*."

The prince and the princess were here. That explained Calum's behavior. Shouldn't royalty stay out of sight and be surrounded by big guards? He glanced around, okay, no one would get to them with the lot that was here.

Calum grinned wide and looked at the floor.

Devin gave him a blank look. "Cal, why don't you introduce everyone—because I think every shifter on the planet knows *you.*"

The smirk left Calum's face as he gave the prince a hard look that promised retribution.

Why didn't it surprise him, that Calum was in with the prince of the shifter world, Deacon wondered?

"*Love* to." Calum finally said, a totally fake smile on his face. "Your highness." He bowed slightly to him. "First and most important is my mate," Calum motioned to the lady with the long black hair sitting in the chair in the corner, "Shaelan. She's our medic, so be nice to her." He looked around the room. "The rest of the retrieval team are," he looked at the tall silent man, "Noah, he has firsthand knowledge of how Tomas works."

Deacon inclined his head as Noah glanced around. He hadn't recognized him at first, but Deacon had been there when they'd gotten him out. He'd put on some weight and looked healthy now. The darkness behind his eyes made sense now. He was a survivor and probably the most important one on this op, he figured, he knew how these sick people operated.

"Blair and his mate, Kobie."

Deacon looked at the couple with almost matching platinum blond hair. Blair didn't smile or acknowledge anyone. His mate leaned into him and rubbed her hand across his chest. Tense didn't even begin to explain the vibes coming from the couple.

"Most of us know Jesse and this is his mate," Calum looked at her and then around at everyone else, "Evanna." He motioned to the two men sitting on the large sectional in the corner. "Bear and Creed."

Deacon noted which was which and then looked back to Calum.

"From Jesse's team we have Webb," the man waved. He pointed to the man beside Deacon, "Asher." Then he looked at Giana, "And Gia, who I'm told out-witted Jesse and Webb today."

Webb shrugged, a big grin on his face.

Jesse rolled his eyes. "Looking *in* the ground never crossed my mind," Jesse said quickly.

Giana wasn't blushing or smiling at any of this. She pulled her hat down further and made no comment. Deacon glanced down at Nox, he looked less than impressed that his sister was mentioned in a positive light.

"That leaves the members of our Incursion team that are here to make sure we all get out in one piece." Calum pointed to the couch, "Nox and York," he motioned to him, "and Deacon."

"I guess the only one left is me, Illias." He waved his hand in the air. "Illias Roman, I'm your tech genius for the foreseeable future."

The room was silent as Calum looked at his phone. "There won't be a second house, so we're going to have to sort out staying here for the next week."

"I'm prepared for that," Rayne slid forward on the sofa. "I did a quick run-through when we got here, just in case."

Calum held his hand toward her to say, 'it's all yours'.

"Okay, we have five bedrooms, a one-bedroom above the garage, and the cute little guest house."

"I'll crash where I'm setting up the equipment." Illias pointed to the door at the top of the stairs he sat on, "I think it's supposed to be a den, but now it's the command center." He grinned.

"Perfect." Rayne smiled at Jesse, "why don't you and Evanna take the guest house."

Jesse looked relieved and nodded.

"Bear, Creed, and Noah, you could use the apartment above the garage."

Devin turned to her; his brows knitted.

She smirked, "I know, but chances of Calum letting you stay where he can't stand guard was slim."

"She's right." Calum gave the prince a quick review.

Rayne gave her mate an 'I told you so' look. "Okay, Webb, Nox, and York, you could take the larger room upstairs. We have sleeping bags on route with the supplies."

Webb nodded, as well as York. Nox didn't look impressed

but shrugged anyway.

"Cal and Shae, Blair and Kobie, and Devin and I will take a room." She looked at Gia, "you could use the smaller one at the back of the kitchen."

Gia nodded.

"So that leaves…"

"I'm going to crash in the van," Asher said. "One of us should stay outside."

Deacon didn't relish the idea of being in this building at all. "I'll take the back shed. As Asher," he glanced at him, "said, we should have some outside keeping an eye on things."

"Okay." Devin nodded, "get your gear to your room, while we get some coffee going and Illias gets set up. Then we hammer out some plans." He looked at Blair, "Lindon's is first."

Blair nodded his head slowly and Deacon didn't know who Lindon was, but he wasn't surviving this if Blair's expression was any clue.

Chapter Seven

Gia stood off to the side, along with Asher and Webb, this part of the planning didn't involve them. When the rest of the team went in, they were a block away and out of sight. Shaelan would be waiting with them in case anyone needed medical attention.

Her heart was beating fast and had been since she realized this first breach, as they'd called it, did not involve rescuing anyone. This first group effort was to stop someone that had been involved with the Tomas organization for years. They were shifters. She was having trouble wrapping her head around the fact that others like herself would willingly help imprison others and destroy so many lines.

"No." Blair's tone cut through her internal chatter, "I don't care what you do with the rest, but he's not being taken into custody."

The room was silent now, all eyes on him.

"Blair," Devin spoke with a soft tone.

"No. Look, I know you want more information, but not from him." Blair paced to the other side of the room, shaking his head, "there's only one way he's coming out of there and he won't have a pulse when he does."

Devin looked over at Calum. The look that passed between them wasn't filled with serious objections.

"He killed my father," Blair looked from Devin to Calum, "and most of Kobie's clan." Shaking his head Blair put his hands on his hips, "he doesn't deserve to breathe another day." Crossing his arms over his chest he stood across the room and glared at the two leaders. "I don't care what you do with the rest of them, but my brother, he dies—" he looked around at a few of the others, "by *my* hand."

Gia was sure she wasn't the only one that sucked in a breath and forgot to release it. His brother?

Jesse cleared his throat and stood up from where he'd been perched on the edge of the table. "Lindon Eldon unlawfully killed the Alpha and assumed control of the clan twenty-one years ago and the clan has since then been assisting the Tomas family to abduct our kind."

The silence in the room was quick. No one moved or spoke. All eyes were on Blair now, even as Kobie went over and stood in front of him. She didn't touch him, wasn't trying to soothe him.

"The only thing he deserves is death," she finally said in a low tone.

Gia was trying to fit together the pieces inside her head, Blair and Kobie were both from Alpha families, she'd heard that from Webb and Asher, so had this Lindon killed both Alphas? She knew clan politics, she should, it had been preached to her for her entire life. "The penalty for unlawfully killing an Alpha without a challenge is death." She said loud enough so others would hear her. She didn't care if she was supposed to be part of this conversation or not. Fact was fact. They had rules they lived by and no one was above them.

Devin and Calum both turned to look at her. She could feel their eyes on her, she knew the others were looking at her too. Taking off her hat, she wanted to be respectful to the prince and maintain eye contact if he spoke to her.

"She's right." Calum finally broke the silence with those two words. "If he challenges Lindon and wins," he glanced at Blair, his mouth shifting like he was suppressing a smirk, "*when* he wins, the fate of those with Lindon becomes Blair's decision."

"You think that group is going to follow clan law?" Devin took a deep breath and studied Blair for a moment. He exhaled then slowly looked around at the rest of the group. "Okay." He looked back at Blair. "Lindon is all yours, but we need as many of the others as possible."

Blair nodded his head once. "I don't care what you do with them. Shoot them for all I care." He moved with brisk movement and went out the back door. His mate watched him leave and then turned to follow him.

Gia blew out a breath and gripped her hat tight in two hands. Many of the others kept looking back at her. Nox gave her a look that told her she should have kept her mouth shut, that it wasn't her place to speak up. She looked away from him and her gaze connected with Deacon. He wasn't judging her as her brother was, he inclined his head to her in a silent acknowledgment that she'd done the right thing. That was twice now in the short time that he'd been on her side. She needed to know more about this large, silent man.

"That brings me to the other thing," Devin turned back to the map, "this area is populated, we can't go in there with guns blazing," he glanced at Illias, "everyone will be carrying a tranq gun." Turning he looked directly at Gia, "even the transport. If anyone comes out of that building that isn't one of us, you knock them out."

"I'll be outside by the fence." Evanna stood up and crossed her arms over her chest. Jesse turned around and looked at her. "I'm not sitting in a van, Jesse, that's not what I signed up to do."

Jesse stood there, looking at his mate like they were silently communicating without a word. Gia even held her breath.

"Leah will be safe," Evanna said, still holding his look.

Kobie stood in the door now, Blair right behind her.

Jesse turned to look at Illias, "give her a tranq gun and a real one."

Illias nodded, "I brought enough toys for everyone."

"Let's take a break, grab a coffee or drink while I check in with the teams watching these places," Devin said as he got up and headed for the stairs. Rayne gave everyone a compassionate glance and followed him.

Gia let out a slow breath, *that happened*, she thought. She looked around, not sure where she could hide to escape the lecture she knew was coming from her brother. Before she could decide on a direction, he blocked her path from going any direction.

"What are you doing?" He hissed. "You are *trans-port*," he waved his hand at the map, "none of this is for you to decide."

Gia glared up at him, "I was just stating the facts. The laws that *all* of us live by." She stepped closer and lifted her chin so he would be sure to see the look in her eyes, "if we don't follow them, then we're no better than those taking our kind."

He gripped her elbow and jerked her arm, so they moved into the hallway and out of sight from the others. "It's still not your place, Giana, you keep your head down, and follow instructions, *nothing...*"

"I know you'd like to whip it out and spray your sister's boots to mark your territory, but we don't have time for this shit."

Nox released her elbow and turned to look at Deacon.

"What did you just say to me?" He stepped away from her and stood a few inches from Deacon, his jaw set, shoulders back. He emitted a low growl.

"She was right to speak up. None of us were thinking clearly right then." Deacon growled low.

Nox bared his teeth, "It's none..."

There was a third growl, "is there a problem here?" Devin's tone sent a chill up her back.

York came over and pushed Nox back.

Gia backed up, looking for a place to escape as Rayne and Devin came down the stairs, "Gia, I could use you up here." Rayne motioned for the stairs. Nodding, she looked at Deacon, not her brother as she turned, his eyes were focused solely on her and not wavering despite whatever Calum was quietly saying to him.

Rolling his head to the side, Deacon spun on his heel and headed for the back door.

Chapter Eight

Deacon stomped down the stairs and kept going, he needed to put as much space between him and Giana right now. His creature was ready to step in and claim her.

"You want to tell me where your heads at, Deacon?"

Just like that his animal settled and he felt like that scrawny, scared kid that Calum had found all over again. Deacon took off his hat and tossed it on the ground, then rubbed his hands through his hair, trailing down his face to his beard. He opened his eyes and looked at the man that had saved him and given him a new lease on life. "She's my mate, Calum." He whispered, feeling the angst and pain flood him as he admitted it out loud for the first time.

"You found out? Just now?"

"No." He shook his head. "No. Remember that call five years ago where I sounded like a complete lunatic?"

Calum grinned, "there's been a few like that, but yeah, I recall it." Putting his hands on his hips, he looked down at the ground. "It makes sense now."

"The call?" Deacon rolled his shoulders trying to release some of the tension from them. He needed a good workout.

"No, why you trained like something unholy possessed

you." Calum came over and leaned against the table, looking relaxed, but Deacon knew better, Calum Dante was never relaxed.

Deacon snorted, "Yeah, well, something does and right now it wants out to claim his mate."

"Do you believe in a deity?"

Deacon snarled, "do you?"

"No." Calum shook his head, "I believe in human nature and animal instinct, one or the other always shows their true intentions." He gave his head a shake like this wasn't the time for a discussion about religious beliefs. "Your animal is not unholy. I've told you that."

Deacon looked back at him, wishing he could feel it like Calum did, "no, just an abomination."

Calum shook his head, an annoyed expression on his face, "no, you are a maned wolf. I would have told you if you'd asked."

"A what?" Deacon looked at him, wondering if he was making it up.

"I traced your history, a long time ago." Cal shrugged.

Deacon couldn't mask his shock.

Calum gave him a hard look, "I wasn't about to let you align yourself with the king and the Alliance if I didn't know your history."

"My father was a fox, my mother was…"

"Just stop blowing hot air for a second and listen." Calum pushed away from the table and came back over to him.

If any other man had said that to Deacon, they would have been chewing on his knuckles through their busted teeth.

"It took a lot of digging and phone calls, to find out, but some of your mother's clan broke off and came across the ocean to live here, in the states, she was a maned wolf. I've seen you shift, Deacon, run with your animal, the only part of your father you got was some of his darker colorings, the rest is a spitting image of your clan."

"I'm still…"

"What? A mix? That happens, not often, but it's not the

first time and won't be the last. Just because there are not twenty clans like you doesn't make you any less a legitimate shifter."

Deacon sucked in a breath and breathed some of the turmoil out, "it doesn't change the fact that she," he pointed to the house, "is an Alpha's daughter and I'm a mangy mutt."

"That is for the two of you to work out, not politics. No father can interfere if their daughter's mate claims them, not even an Alpha." He smirked, "and I don't know if you noticed, but Gia, she has a mind of her own, and no posturing, permission, or social dictating stops her from doing what her heart and head tell her to do."

"*Fuck.* Just *fuck.*"

Calum grinned, "I know that chant well." He smacked him on the shoulder, "just keep your shit together so we can get through this. With Blair and Noah in on this, did you see the look in their eyes at the mention of Lindon?"

"Yeah, I caught the vibes." He gave his head a slight shake, trying to focus, "Wynter told us the first one was straight takedown though, so I wasn't shocked."

"Yeah, the first stop is paying a visit to his brother, and I'll tell you right now, it's going to be fast and violent."

Deacon rolled his shoulders, "I could use a little of smacking traitors around right now."

Calum chuckled, "I think we all do."

They both turned to watch Evanna walking quickly to the guest house.

Deacon didn't know if he should ask or if it would be considered disrespectable. "Calum?" He waited until he looked back at him. "Jesse's mate—" How did he word this?

"Oh," Calum glanced at the house briefly, "if her hair is down," he motioned to his own shoulder, "call her Leah, and don't approach her without Jesse or one of the women nearby."

Deacon gave him a look and was going to clarify the name, but Calum continued.

"If her hair is pulled up, it's Evanna, and don't sneak up on her if she has a gun." He smirked, "if her cat comes out because you've upset either, be somewhere else, *fast*." Calum turned and walked back toward the house without another word.

Deacon didn't have time to figure out what *that* was about. He paced to the back of the yard, as far as he could without pressing his nose against the fence itself. He had to get his head together. This was too important. There were too many lives at stake here, not just his mate, but families, and shifters that were captives. Deacon may not be from a perfect clan, but these were his people too.

"Deacon."

Turning, he saw York and Nox walking toward him quickly. Neither looked happy.

Going over, he picked up his hat, ready to settle this once and for all.

York stopped and held up his phone. "We're with Deacon now."

"What the actual hell was that shit?"

Deacon's eyes widened when he heard his own team leader's unhappy tone coming through the speaker.

"Don't even try some suck-up bullshit, Nox—I was on the phone with Devin, our prince, as he stood there watching it." Wynter growled in frustration, "I know it's just some pent-up testosterone kind of shit because you're sitting idle but put a cork in it—I won't have members of *my* team pulling that drama *BS* again. Solid?"

All three of them nodded.

"I asked if we were solid."

"Completely," York said quickly.

"Got it, Boss." Nox added.

"Solid." Deacon whispered, knowing even over the phone she'd hear him.

"Good. Now hang up the phone and go be fucking team players together."

York hung up and looked from one to the other. "What the hell, guys?"

Nox glared at Deacon then spun back toward the house.

York shook his head and looked back to Deacon.

Taking off his hat, he smoothed the long hair on top of his head back and put the hat over it. "Just going stir crazy."

York nodded, "I get that, but dial it back, okay? I do not want my ass on Wynter's shit list or to look like an idiot to the prince."

"Yeah, sorry." He watched York walk away. He had no problem apologizing to York, Nox on the other hand—that wasn't going to happen, not with the way he'd treated Gia.

Taking a deep breath, he tried to settle some of the chaos in his mind. The taste of jasmine hit his tongue, lifting his head, he watched Gia walk across the yard. His animal settled, which concerned him more than if it had been raging. The last five feet felt like it took an eternity. He debated on jumping the fence, rather than doing something epically stupid and ultimately embarrassing.

She took off her hat and looked up at him. "I just wanted to say thank you."

Deacon was struck by her eyes; he'd never seen them this close before. From a distance, they were grey but up close, they had golden flecks in them, and he couldn't look away.

"No one has ever done something like that for me."

His brain cued him that she was waiting for him to acknowledge that she'd spoken to him. "It wasn't right for him to get all up in your face." Was the best he could come up with. His creature was just as stunned as he was right now, her scent, being this close— He backed up a few steps and looked at the shed, he couldn't get too close to her.

"We've met before."

He cleared his throat, of all the things to talk about, this would have been the last thing he would have picked. "Yeah— I was, I should apologize for being an ass back then."

Flipping her hair back from her face, she shrugged, "A boy acting like a pompous jerk is something I'm used to." She motioned to the house, "you've met one of my brothers, there's more like him."

"I'm sorry about that." He grinned fleetingly. His eyes were memorizing her face while she stood so close. The trace of freckles across the bridge of her nose made him want to kiss them, taste them. He took a step back so he wouldn't act on his thoughts.

The smile on her face faded. "This uh, team is quite the mix."

"The ops," he could talk about that. It was a safe topic. "It's long overdue—taking action."

Gia nodded and wrapped her arms around her waist, "I think so too. I've heard of so many being taken; it has to be stopped."

"We'll do that."

"I've only been on the coordinator's team for a few weeks." She bit her lip.

"You wouldn't be here if they didn't think you couldn't do it." He motioned to the house, "Calum and Jesse picked everyone here."

They both watched Evanna come out of the guest house, gone were her jeans, and instead, she was wearing a long skirt. Her hair was down. He frowned, so she was no longer Evanna? He really needed to clarify that with Calum. Looking back down at her, he saw the look in her eyes change, it was harder now. Something had changed in the last few moments. His creature wanted him to move closer, to take her scent into their body. Deacon crossed his arms over his chest so he wouldn't reach out and touch her.

"Are you really going to sleep in the shed?"

Ignoring his animal, he nodded. "Yeah, there's too many walls and bodies to stay there." He jerked his chin toward the house.

"It is crowded." She said in a quiet voice. "I should uh, get back. They're going to pair everyone up." She grimaced, "if I know my brother, he's in there pushing to be with me."

The anxiety coming off her almost choked him, "I'm sure..."

"Deacon. Gia." Jesse stood on the deck. "You two are partnering up. From now on you're her shadow, Deacon." He opened the door again, "Illias is going over the gear now." He went back in.

She turned and looked back up at him, something was going through her mind, and he couldn't catch the expressions flashing through her eyes. "We should, uh," she motioned to the house.

He lurched, "Yeah, we should get back in there." He nodded.

Her eyes searched his for a moment then she turned and started walking.

Deacon stood there—froze on the spot, how the hell was he going to stand working closely with her? He couldn't even breathe around her. Glancing at the fence again, he debated if he should have jumped it and run. He started walking, then spotted Calum standing in the window looking out at him. Blowing out a breath, he looked at the grass ahead of him. If this was some sort of test, he was going to fail. There was no way he could be this close to Giana all the time and not come off as some sort of a jerk. He needed to be though; it was for her own good. She was out to prove to her brother—he frowned, brothers most likely, that she belonged in this type of life. The last thing she needed was some mangy mutt, who happened to be her mate, claiming her.

Chapter Nine

Gia sat on the window ledge and looked down over the new neighborhood being constructed. There were so many houses, most in the final stages of construction. She hadn't expected this to be part of what she was to do, but the surveillance team had been pulled to go monitor other places. She knew too many people affected by the organization that had wreaked havoc and heartache in their world for years—she'd do whatever was required of her to help.

She didn't know why her new partner had chosen the building location instead of being closer and observing from the van, but now that she'd sat here for three hours, she was glad he had, she would have gone stir crazy sitting in the confines of a vehicle doing nothing.

The building they were watching from was a partially constructed apartment building. According to Illias, construction was currently on hold, so it was abandoned and a perfect site to see the comings and goings from a house a few blocks over, in the house was one of the team's brothers and remaining traitorous clan members. She no longer questioned why they would do something like that, it didn't matter now. This Lindon person was responsible for the captures, or worse of Kobie's clan members. The fact that Blair was going to kill his brother for his crimes against their people was sitting better than she had ever thought something like that would. She just hoped she did her part without issue, she refused to be the weak link with the team.

Looking at Deacon, he hadn't moved more than an inch since the last time she'd glanced in his direction. He was at the far end of the empty room, standing by a dirty window, his eyes trained on the building they were to watch. Was it part of their training to withstand long hours of no movement, or was it just a part of him that allowed him to not have to fidget and move around? Sitting still had never been something she was good at.

The radio he'd set on the ledge squawked. "Delivery truck pulling in." He tilted his head, keeping his eyes trained on the location.

Their eyesight allowed them to see further, but Gia still felt the need to pick up the small binoculars and look at the house's driveway. "That's the third one if you count the takeout order and pharmacy." She didn't look away, "why would shifters need a pharmacy?" She hadn't expected a reply, so his voice breaking the silence startled her.

"They shouldn't unless someone is seriously injured."

Lowering the cool metal from her face, she looked over at him. "According to the other team, they haven't gone anywhere in several days, how would someone get injured?"

"Their timeline has seven of them going out last week and only six returning, one was limping when they helped him back into the house."

"It would have to be serious enough that they couldn't shift." She'd only experienced that once in her clan, a broken bone being the cause.

"One less to worry about."

His tone wasn't cold exactly, and he was just stating the facts, but it still bothered her to think that parts of this new team were going to potentially be hurt taking this clan into custody.

"Truck is leaving. Four mid-sized boxes were left outside the garage door. No contact with anyone inside." York's steady tone reported.

"Get pictures of whoever brings them in." That was Jesse. She hadn't realized the others back at the house were listening in.

"Webb's ready with the camera to send it back to you, Jesse."

Deacon moved and picked up his binoculars and lifted them.

Gia turned back to the window and found where the boxes were sitting. She held her breath when the garage door opened slowly. As the man appeared in the opening, she sucked in a breath, he looked almost the same as Blair, older, but there was no mistaking they were related.

"It's Lindon, himself carrying them in," York told everyone listening.

"Bingo." Illias' voice came over the radio.

"There you are." Deacon said in a soft tone.

Lowering the binoculars, she looked over at him. "They've been waiting to confirm he was there, haven't they?"

"Yeah. He hasn't been seen since they returned." He looked over at her for the first time since they'd been here."

"York, you and Webb stay put. Deacon and Gia, head back now." Devin's voice cut into the silence.

Deacon moved back from the window and went over and picked up the radio. "We're on the way."

Gia looked out the window again quickly, then back to him. "I want to drive the neighborhood and get a feel for it."

Deacon's look assessed her for a moment. She couldn't be sure, but it looked like approval on his face. "We're going to do a run through the area and check alternate routes on the way." He reported.

"Sounds good." Calum's even tone replied.

Clipping the radio to the front of his vest, he motioned to the door, then stood there unmoving waiting for her to go.

"We'll be going in soon now, won't we?" She thought she'd

feel dread of what was to come, but it wasn't hitting her as hard as she thought it would.

He nodded, "They were just waiting to confirm Lindon was there, so yeah it will go fast now before they have a chance to leave."

An anxious feeling ran through her. "I'm nervous," she admitted.

The tense lines on his face eased, "that's good, it's better than being cocky. Nervous keeps you aware and ready."

Gia blew out a breath, then gave him a small smile. "Thanks for that."

He nodded, then motioned to the door, "let's go, by the time we get back, they'll have a plan."

She turned the corner and glanced over at him. He had the window down all the way again, uncaring of the cool air. "You don't like feeling confined, do you?"

He looked over at her for a second before answering. "No. I grew up mostly outdoors," he shrugged, "except the odd time we found somewhere to crash."

"Your clan moved around a lot?" She turned her attention back to the road, noting the side streets along the way.

"This street is too bogged." He said in a flat tone.

Nodding, she'd just been thinking the same thing. Checking the mirror, she switched lanes and turned at the next intersection. She looked over to see him take off his hat and rest it on his knee.

"I wasn't part of a clan." He said finally.

Gia had to work hard to not look at him with her mouth hanging open. "You're," *how was that possible? He worked for the Alliance.* "You're not?"

His steel-colored eyes locked with hers before she forced them to look back to the road. "No. Surprised? I'm sure all Alpha families talk about the rogue wanderers out there."

"Uh, yeah, we're aware they exist. I think all our kind are." She gripped the steering wheel harder and watched where she was driving.

"Well, now you've met one of the rogues." His tone was flat. "I'm a nobody, the equivalent of the runt of the litter."

Gia snorted and looked over at him, making sure he saw her check him over. "Yeah, you're a runt if King Kong had siblings."

His grin was quick. "No siblings." He finally said.

"I'm just surprised," she had to explain her reaction, she didn't want him to think she was judging him, "your part of one of the Alliance teams," she glanced at him again quickly, without his hat he looked completely different. The sides of his head were shaved, but the top of his hair was quite long, now falling to the one side of his face, down to his jaw. "How did that happen?"

"Calum." He said it like the one-word answer would explain it all.

"Calum got you in?" She shrugged, "I suppose if someone could, it's him."

"He found me." Deacon looked out the side window, "in an old hunter's shack in the middle of nowhere." He ran his fingers over his beard, a look on his face that told her he was remembering then. "Even with his help, it was a long road to where I am now."

"I would imagine it's a hard task for anyone to get on the team." She tried to recall if Nox had worked hard at it or if his status had given him a free pass. They'd never gotten along, so she couldn't be sure.

"It was hard, I did a few years of bowing my head a lot proving myself loyal before I ever got the chance to try for anything." His voice was quiet, which surprised her, she would have been spiteful as hell if she'd had to prove herself to anyone like that.

"Well," she looked over and gave him a quick smile, "I guess you were found worthy, or you wouldn't be here."

He didn't reply or smile, just studied her face for a moment and gave her a slight nod.

"I think this street is the one. Only two stop signs." She had to try to bring the conversation around to something that didn't make her chest feel tight. Why it was, she wasn't sure. Could it be the injustice of his life or the fact she was trapped in her own? Licking her lips, she checked all the mirrors while trying to find something to break the awkward silence. "So, uh, what's it like not having a clan and all the rules? Who leads and makes decisions?"

Deacon turned back to look at her, his eyes holding her own. "It's a consensus thing, how decisions are made."

Gia looked away again, "that must be nice. Not being dictated to."

"Are you thinking of leaving your clan?" He smirked at her.

She blew out a breath, was she? "I'd consider it, maybe, if it wouldn't break my mother's heart." She gave him a blank look. "Youngest of five and only female child." She supplied so he would have the context to understand her position.

"Five kids are a lot."

"Yes, it is," she shrugged, "I don't know what it's like with sisters, maybe it's different, but I've had four older brothers and a father, dictating to me for as long as I can remember," she shrugged, "except Walker, he's not too bad."

"You don't strike me as someone who likes to be told what to do."

She looked quickly at him; he wasn't smirking at all. "You would be right." She cleared her throat, "I took self-defense, weapon training," she sighed, "everything that was expected of my brothers and handed to them," she gripped the steering wheel, "*but* I had to do it in secret."

"Sometimes you just have to do what your heart tells you, and to hell with those that stand in your way."

He said that like he'd lived it too at some point. "Exactly. So here I am." She turned her head to look at him again, "And I don't need the macho man routine, by the way, I can take care of myself."

Deacon lifted his hands like he was surrendering, "you are definitely nothing like your kin," he smirked at her finally, "and don't worry I won't tell Nox a thing."

Gia looked at him twice, before answering, just to be sure he was being serious. "Thank you." She nodded, "And I don't care where you're from or about your past, Deacon, that's not who I am. I judge a person on who they are now." She slowed down out front of the house they were staying at, then glanced at the clock. "Twenty-six minutes, if we're coming back here," she shrugged, "less because we won't be circling the neighborhood."

"We won't be bringing anyone back here." He motioned to the fence. "I'll get the gate." He opened the door and paused, "our location is only to be known to us." He got out and jogged over to the fence.

Gia bit her lip, then blew out a slow breath. That whole conversation had been a surprise. She never would have imagined he had no clan. He was so disciplined and considerate, the sort of thing she expected from someone with a good upbringing. Her parents had gone on and on about the lawlessness of rogue wanderers, but Deacon didn't fit the profile she'd pictured at all. Pulling the van in behind the fence, she pulled it up as far as she could, not knowing when the others would be back. Her whole life had been about family and clan ties, what had it been like for him? She couldn't even picture it and didn't want to bring it up again because he looked like he was in his own personal hell for a few moments during the conversation.

Getting out, she closed the door and then turned to see him watching her, his hat back on, his eyes shadowed by the bill of it. "After we find out what's going on, would you be able to take a few minutes to explain the dart gun to me?"

He tilted his head but didn't speak.

"It doesn't shoot the same as normal ones and I don't want to miss anyone if I need to use it."

Rubbing his hand over his beard brusquely he finally nodded, "Yeah, we can go over it," he patted the one sticking out of a holder on the front of his vest, "if we do our job, you won't need to use it at all."

"Better safe than sorry." She nodded, then motioned to the

house. "I need to keep moving so my nerves don't get the better of me." Gia didn't know why she admitted that to him. Afraid of the reasons, she quickly walked in the direction of the house. They needed to get moving on these plans, or she wasn't going to talk herself right out of doing the job she was chosen to do.

Chapter Ten

"In two hours when it's dark, we're going in. Illias has some items for each of you. Before you head out, pack up your stuff and take it with you."

"Aren't we coming back here?" Webb interrupted Calum.

Gia watched Devin and Calum exchange a look.

"That's the plan but being prepared for any situation never hurts."

She gnawed on her lower lip; did they expect something to happen that would mean they weren't coming back here?

"Best case scenario, you'll already be packed to move to the other safe house."

"We'll be staggering the times of everyone leaving throughout the night and early morning." Devin looked around at everyone, "but we'll cover that when you're back." He turned and looked at Illias.

Illias stood up, "everyone is getting a new untraceable phone. Do not use your personal phones if these are activated."

"When will that be?" Kobie moved closer to Blair, who automatically put his arm around her shoulders.

"If anything happens or I think we've been compromised,

I'll put a call out over the radio. Five minutes from that time the radio frequency will be changed so you won't be able to use it after that."

Asher glanced over at Jesse, "will instructions be given at that point?"

Illias nodded after seeking Devin's approval to continue. "Yes. Very brief ones." He held up a phone, "these are for calls only, no texting, no group chats or online surfing, just calls. The fewer the better."

Calum pushed away from the wall, "over the radio or with the new phones, you don't mention where you're going, where you are, nothing personal or identifying." He motioned to the phone Illias held, "once you've been told to use the new phones, you take the chip out of your personal ones and power them off." He paused to look around at everyone in the room, "and they don't get turned back on until you're told. Put the new phone in your run pack and leave it there."

Rayne came in with a cup in her hand and sat beside Devin. "This is all a precaution." She smiled at Devin, then Calum, "they forgot to mention that part."

Devin shook his head, and smirked, but didn't comment. He turned to Illias.

Illias nodded, "each driver is going to be given an envelope, in it is a location of a vehicle you will pick up. These are not traceable in any way." He smirked, "Nola from *my* team has made sure of that. The only one that knows who is picking up which vehicle is me." He pointed to the scar on his face, "and I don't share information—ever."

"While you hand out the phones and envelopes, we'll go over the task at hand." Calum looked to Jesse, then Devin, both men seemed okay with him continuing.

Gia watched Illias go over and pick up a small box sitting on the floor. Her heart was racing, not from fear, but from adrenalin. She was finally going to do something to contribute to the Alliance and her kind.

"While everyone is moving into position, Creed is going to do a quick flyover and check that things haven't changed, in case Noah isn't able to follow movement in the back of the location."

Gia looked around; she hadn't noticed that Noah was missing.

Shaelan grinned and held up a radio, "he's listening, so he knows when we're moving."

"If Creed doesn't land, drive away and wait for further instructions." Calum turned to Webb, "Webb, you're waiting here," he pointed to a spot on the map, "you'll drop off Blair, Kobie, Jesse, and Evanna. They're coming in from the back."

Webb nodded and took the radio, phone, and envelope that Illias handed him.

"Asher," Calum paused while he was handed him his items, "Bear and Creed will ride with you. Let Creed out here and wait for his signal, then you'll pick up Noah, he's here," he showed him on the map. "You'll drop them off at this corner and then go wait at the location of your choosing.

Asher looked at the map for a moment, his expression tense. Nodding, he backed out of the way again.

"Gia," she stood up and went closer to the map, "you're going to have Shaelan with you," he glanced at his mate, "we'll load up any supplies in your van after this." He turned and looked around, "Shae has an additional bag for you to keep in the vehicles as well," when Asher and Webb nodded, he turned back to her, "you'll drop Deacon off," she watched where he pointed "then I want you to stay the closest in case we need Shaelan."

Illias came over and handed her a radio, a small black phone, and an envelope. She took them and then looked at Calum again. "Got it." She answered, keeping words few so the shakiness she was feeling wouldn't be evident. Moving out of the way, she watched as he moved through the room and handed the others their items.

"Bear, once Asher drops you off, can you disable the vehicles sitting in the driveway?" Calum smirked, "but make sure they can be loaded or towed after."

Bear grinned, "I can do that."

Calum looked around at everyone. "We have extra darts and ammo for everyone. Let's try not to fire any guns and alert the entire neighborhood to what's happening." He turned and looked at Devin.

Devin stood up again, "I'll be taking Illias to the house five minutes before the rest of you so he can check for and disable any security systems."

Illias paused in handing Deacon his items, "I also have a neat toy that will turn off the automatic garage door." He grinned, then continued with what he'd been doing.

"I'll be at the location with Devin and Illias and waiting on your arrival. Keep the chatter down on the radios, only necessary information." Calum nodded slowly as he looked at each person present.

Jesse moved from Evanna's side and put his hands on his hips, "the security team's location is only known to Devin, Calum, and I, so once we've dealt with Lindon, any others will be taken to them to be moved."

York took his new phone and radio, then looked over to Deacon, "are we expecting them to come willingly?"

Jesse shrugged, "if not, tranq them for transport. The Alliance security are better equipped to deal with them."

York nodded and moved to the other end of the room, to the table with the clips and darts on it. He picked up one of each and tucked them into the pockets of his cargo pants.

"Any questions?" Calum looked around at everyone. When no one spoke, he motioned to the table of ammo. "Get your gear packed up and put in the vehicle you'll be riding in."

Going over, Gia quickly picked up the ammo and added it to the other items in her hand. She moved through the kitchen into the room she'd been assigned. There wasn't much for her to pack, she'd left most of her belongings in the van. Setting the things down on the bed, she looked down at them for a moment. The envelope and new phone were going right into her run pack.

"Gia."

She spun around to see Nox standing inside the room. She braced herself for what she knew was coming.

"If anything goes down, you get to me immediately."

She wanted to argue, to tell him she'd be following whatever instructions she was given but knew that would just result in another dramatic scene and she was done with those. Nodding quickly, she watched him look her up and down and then turn and leave the room.

Jesse stepped into the doorway as soon as he was gone. "I've asked Devin to replace your brother with another member of the incursion team after this." He gave her a slow appraisal, "the others are busy elsewhere, so he can't for a few days."

Gia felt her shoulders relax. "Thank you." She looked out the door to be sure her brother wasn't lurking. "I will follow instructions if anything happens."

Jesse smirked, "I figured that. I have two sisters; I know a brush-off when I see one."

She smiled, "they're lucky to have you. I hope you don't try to control their lives."

Jesse crossed his arms over his chest and leaned against the door, "there is no force on earth that could control those two." He grinned, "they're twins, and, in the future, I feel like they're going to blaze a trail of broken rules."

Gia tucked her hoodie into the bag and then looked at him, "nothing wrong with stretching a few rules here and there." She zipped up the bag, "if we have to use those new phones," she didn't want to say out loud if something goes wrong, "can I call my one brother quickly before turning mine off?"

Jesse rubbed a hand over his jaw, "very quickly and give no information."

She nodded, "thank you. It's just so he can let my mother know I'm all right."

Nodding, he glanced back out the door, "get loaded up, grab some extra supplies from the garage. There's jerky, juice, bars, and a few other things."

Gia inhaled a deep breath and exhaled slowly. "Jesse," he

glanced back at her, "thank you, for having me on the team."

"Amari gave me raving reviews about you," he gave her a wide-eyed look, "and she doesn't approve of most, so that told me that this is where you needed to be."

She watched him walk away, then jumped and looked around the room. Her nerves felt like they were live wires in her body. "Nervous is good." She whispered, remembering what Deacon had told her. Taking the ammo, she tucked it into the other bag Illias had given her earlier. Her weapon bag… She had a weapon bag.

Going out through the kitchen, she noticed everyone was in motion, things being packed or carried, and the whole team seemed like they had been activated at once. There were no smiles, no banter or chatter, just focus.

As she stepped outside, she watched Deacon come across the yard carrying his bag and gear. He didn't seem nervous at all, in fact, his expression wasn't any different than it had been prior to the planning discussion. She motioned to the van when he looked up and noticed her, "I can put your gear in if you want to go grab extra supplies from the garage."

He paused in step and then nodded, "I'll give Shaelan a hand bringing her stuff out first."

Gia tried to keep a smile on her face, but she wasn't feeling it right now, so again she just nodded and turned to go to the van.

"Giana."

She turned back to look at him. She hated her given name, but the way it sounded from him made it seem special. Then again, any other time it was said, the person saying it was going to tell her what to do.

He offered her a soft look, it even reached his eyes, taking the toothpick out of his mouth, he smiled slowly, "it's going to be fine." He set his bag down, "you just have to have faith it will go off without a hitch."

Huffing out a breath she nodded again, "but be prepared for sudden changes."

He smiled again, "exactly." Winking at her, he put the

toothpick back in his mouth and walked toward the deck.

"Have faith," she whispered, "faith in myself, faith in my team," she watched him go in the house, "faith he will watch my back." Blowing out a breath, she went over to grab his gear. She was torn between having a nervous breakdown and fist-pumping in the air. This was so much more than she thought she'd be doing on the co-ord team. This was being on the front lines, so to speak, being right there when people from her world were rescued. "Let's do it."

Chapter Eleven

"Here's good." Deacon didn't wait for the vehicle to come to a complete stop before he opened the door and checked the street before hopping out. "Stay close." He put his earpiece in and looked back at the two women in the van. Shaelan was already moving to open a case and was hanging up an IV bag. Turning his hat around backward, he looked around. Creed was in his bird form and sitting on the end of the fence, the streetlight shining down on him. "If you see that bird," he motioned to him with his hand as he made eye contact with Giana, "swoop down in front of the van, get out of here, it means someone is coming." He made sure she acknowledged and then closed the door quickly.

Deacon didn't look back to watch the van leave, he just moved fast into the shadows of the buildings. He spotted Calum crouched down beside a garden shed near the fence that separated the properties. Bear was a few feet from him, trying to keep his large body out of the illumination of the streetlights.

He knew York was somewhere nearby but didn't pause to pinpoint his location. That went for Nox as well. He may be an overbearing jerk to his sister, but he was good at his job.

Calum looked over at him and nodded his head. Deacon

66

felt a flush of pride move through him. To have Calum, of all people telling him to lead on something like this when he was involved, was pure gratification. Calum had always had faith in him, even when he had none in himself.

He touched his earpiece, "moving to disable the cars and breach garage." He turned the mic back off.

"At the back door." Jesse's whisper came over the comm.

"We'll give you the go once we're in." Calum's calm voice came through the earpiece.

Deacon stayed low and moved along the fence until he reached the edge of the driveway. He felt someone move up beside him. Inhaling their scent, he identified it to be Bear. When this was over, he really needed to make inquiries as to what clan Bear was from, because he knew it wasn't any of the *bear* clans.

He pointed to the closest truck in the drive and felt Bear move away from him. With the tranq gun in his hand now, he kept it aimed toward the door of the house.

Someone tapped him on the shoulder twice, telling him either Nox or York would take this position and allow him to move to a closer vantage point.

Deacon moved along the fence and stayed low as he went past the garage door. Once he reached the steps to the front door, he hunkered down and kept his eyes on the part of the door where the frame and actual door connected.

He heard movement behind him but didn't so much as blink. He would only have a split second to react if that door moved and that left no time to look away. Inhaling, he pegged Calum as he moved silently by him. In the year's Deacon had known him, he'd aspired to learn how to move without sound as his large friend and mentor did. He'd managed it eventually, and was almost invisible and unheard, but could never get as good as Calum. Deacon had to wonder if it was because of Calum's cat he was able to do it. Deacon's animal was not sleek and graceful in any way.

"Vehicles disabled." Nox reported.

Nodding to no one in particular, Deacon moved to the

bottom step and went up them with a swift movement. Calum came up beside him. The other two from his team, Deacon knew would be at the garage door.

"Breaching in three." York's steady voice came through the earpiece.

"Two."

Deacon straightened and aligned his body with the side of the door the handle was on.

"One. Now."

Sucking in a breath, Deacon used all his strength and kicked the door right above the handle. Wood cracked under the force and Calum moved to brace the door open as Deacon raised the gun again. With a nod, he told Calum to go in. He followed right behind him, looking in whatever direction Calum wasn't.

As Calum checked, then moved past an open doorway, Deacon moved up to replace him. A movement out of the corner of his eye was the only warning he had before he turned and blocked someone swinging something at his head from around the corner. Grasping the crutch from the man's hand, he jerked it from the other man's hand and shot him in the chest with a dart.

The only thing the guy had time to do was look down at the dart sticking out of his chest, then he slumped to the floor unconscious. How the hell strong were these darts Illias gave them?

Squatting down, Deacon checked his pulse, while keeping his eyes and gun pointed back into the entranceway. Bear came into the room. Deacon stood up. "Carry him out to Shaelan," he motioned to his leg wrapped in bandages, "stay with him and tranq him again if he comes to."

Bear nodded and moved behind him, making sure not to obstruct Deacon's line of sight.

He waited until the large man moved back to the door. Bear moved with fluid steps, making it look like he was carrying a tiny child instead of the dead weight of a knocked-out man.

"Leg injury coming out, Shaelan." He said quietly into the mic, then moved into the room the man had been in. Moving just his eyes, he cleared the room and went toward the open door on the other side.

"Basement cleared," York announced.

Movement from behind him had him spin toward it. It was Blair and Kobie. He lowered the gun. Kobie was armed with her dart gun, Blair had no weapon and only wore a pair of black track pants.

Deacon caught his eye and jerked his chin toward the door he was going to go in. There was a loud thud and then a crash from the space above the room, but he was trained to not be distracted from his task unless someone called it over the radio.

Blair kept his body between the door and Kobie as Deacon reached it and leaned to slowly check one side, and then the other. A man was standing, leaning against the kitchen counter with a beer bottle in his hand. Deacon didn't need to pause to figure out who he was. A little shorter and several years older than Blair, but there was no mistaking the resemblance. His hair was just as light as Blair's but longer and pulled back into a ponytail behind his head.

Lindon Eldon grinned slowly, "Hello, brother. I've been looking forward to meeting you."

Deacon heard a low feral growl from behind him.

"And you've brought your *lovely* mate." Lindon tilted his head to the side, "you did well, keeping her from me."

Deacon had to wonder if this idiot was aware that he was signing his death sentence or if he was that cocky, that he thought he was going to get out of this alive.

Kobie moved past Deacon and stepped in front of him. She raised a real gun and pressed it against the side of Lindon's face. "Outside."

Raising his hands, grin still on his face, Lindon turned toward the back door.

"Moving Lindon out back." Deacon announced to the others.

"We'll bring his five friends out." Calum's calm voice told him.

"Evanna," Jesse's voice was quiet and calm, "Minn, and

Leah cannot watch this."

"I need a hand here," Shaelan's voice was easily recognized. "This leg is an infected mess and Gia needs to stay at the wheel."

Deacon kept his eyes on Lindon, despite Kobie keeping the gun tip pressed against his shoulder as they went out the door.

"I'll go help Shaelan." Deacon was relieved to hear Evanna say. He had *no* idea who Minn was, but he was starting to understand who Leah was and he had to agree with her mate. Leah seemed like a gentle soul and what was about to happen, she should not witness.

Deacon moved out around Lindon, putting himself between him and the fence. He didn't know how fast he could shift or move, and he wasn't taking any chances. His hand itched to pull out his lethal gun and shoot Lindon. He knew the damage he'd done to his own kind; he couldn't imagine what Blair felt, what his mate, Kobie, was feeling.

Nox came out the door and stood to the side of it as Jesse and Calum brought five other men out, two of them stumbled down the steps, but no one moved to help them.

Nox moved back to allow the others to line up the men. York went toward the back fence and positioned himself so no one could make a move toward it.

Deacon watched Calum walk around behind Blair, he expected him to intercede, but his mentor's eyes were locked on Lindon. He kept going until he was standing on the other side of Deacon, where he stopped and crossed his arms over his chest.

Kobie lowered the gun and carefully switched it out for the tranq gun again.

The air was filled with tension, Deacon could taste it. Lindon's men looked confused, to say the least as they peered from their leader to Blair.

"Stay out of it," Lindon said quietly, no longer smiling.

One of his men started to move toward him, obviously not caring about the armed people standing around him. Deacon lifted his hand and landed a dart in his chest. "He said to stay out of it." The man dropped to the ground. Deacon glanced at Calum, who was shaking his head, a half-smirk on his face. Deacon shrugged.

Creed swooped down and circled the group, then flew up and landed on the roof. "All clear," Jesse said in a hushed tone.

Deacon looked to Blair; he hadn't moved a muscle since coming outside. His chest rose and fell in a slow rhythm as he stood there looking at his brother.

"You killed our family, our clan," Blair's voice was more animal than man, "my mates' clan."

Lindon stepped a few feet back, no one moved to stop him. "Our father wouldn't listen..."

"He was the Alpha." Blair's voice trembled with rage.

"He was going to pass me over and hand the clan over to his infant son." Lindon grabbed his shirt and ripped it over his head. He glanced at the four men watching, "you would have been led by a child."

Deacon looked away long enough to note the surprise on the men that had followed the wrong brother for so many years.

"The penalty for unlawful attack on an Alpha, more than one," Calum said in a steady voice, loud enough that the shifters present would hear, "is death." He finished and looked at Blair, "to be carried out by a true Alpha."

One of the men Jesse was holding a gun on dropped to his knees and lowered his head. Deacon almost felt sorry for him, he was asking for forgiveness he would never receive.

Kobie moved quickly and went over to him, grabbing his hair she jerked his head up. She leaned down and made a point of letting everyone know she was inhaling his scent. Releasing his head, she shot him with a dart and then stepped back to look at her mate.

Lindon turned from her to Blair. "Your mate is glorious, brother."

"You are *not* my brother. You belong to no family, no clan." Blair still hadn't moved.

Lindon's expression darkened, "If I best you, they're just

going to shoot me." He lifted his hands out from his body.

"No one will interfere." Blair turned his head and looked at Calum. "If you live through this, you will be put to trial in front of the Alliance.

Calum didn't hesitate or speak, just motioned to the traitor standing before them.

Lindon stripped quickly as if suddenly realizing the dire situation he was in.

Blair made no move at all.

When Lindon stepped back and shifted fast, Blair stood there looking at the large white tiger in front of him. His coat wasn't smooth and there were a lot of scars. The evidence of the fights he'd been in while taking his own kind and turning them over to Tomas couldn't have been clearer.

Lindon hunched down like he was going to lunge for Blair, Deacon's hand went to his regular gun. Calum reached over and clamped his hand over it, preventing him from drawing.

Deacon looked over at him, Calum shook his head and moved his hand.

The animal jumped at Blair and Deacon almost swallowed his tongue when Blair was able to take the brunt of the hit and stay standing. Lindon hit the ground and landed on his side when Blair shoved him back.

Blair's track pants were gone, and a large sleek white tiger stood where he had. He stalked toward his brother with slow steps.

When Lindon stood up, Blair's cat had almost a foot in length and a lot more weight on him. His older brother looked like a second-rate wannabe next to Blair.

From that point on everything was a white blur. After five attempts Lindon still hadn't landed a single blow on Blair, but his white coat was spotted with red streaks.

Lindon flipped and got out from beneath Blair and reared on his back legs, hoping to land a hit on his younger brother. Blair lashed out with sharp claws and got him right along the underbelly, at the same moment he clamped his teeth into his throat.

Deacon held his breath, as Blair with a strength that shocked him, flipped the other cat over him onto the ground—without breaking his hold on his neck. Lindon was trying to spin out of his grip, swatting with his paws and hitting thin air. He'd seen some fights in his life, but not like this and never between two cats of that size. It was a silent, meticulous battle and Lindon was not coming out of it alive.

The cat beneath Blair managed to get his back legs under him and was trying to pull himself free now, only ensuring that his younger siblings' teeth were sinking deeper. Deacon could smell the blood, and there was a lot of it.

Lindon dropped the length of his body to the ground, his sides were heaving in slow deep breaths, like he was struggling to get air.

Blair released him and stood over him, staring down at him. He stepped back, never taking his eyes off him, and then shifted back to skin and went over to his brother's cat laying there on the ground, he was barely breathing now. As he dropped down to one knee, Lindon lashed out with a large paw and slashed Blair's chest.

Grabbing the paw, Blair pinned it to the ground. Leaning down, he said something close to the dying cat's face. Lindon shifted back to the body of a man. Blood from his injuries covered him. With a lightning-fast move, Blair grabbed his head and twisted it. The sound of his neck snapping echoed in the silence.

Getting to his feet slowly, Blair turned around and walked with steady steps to where there other four men stood. "Surrender or run." Blair growled, his chest rising and falling fast, "I love the chase." He added with a tone that sent a chill down Deacon's spine.

The four men looked at Blair for a moment, taking in the blood running down his chest from the claw marks. One by one they raised their hands slowly.

Stepping back, Blair took the pants that Kobie held out to him. She moved to check his bloodied chest, "Leave it." He told her with a gentle tone.

Deacon snapped his head around, remembering they had to get out of here. "Coming out through the garage." He told the others waiting. "Bring the other vans closer." Moving over, he opened the door leading through the garage.

"Send the clean-up here, Devin, and get them to go through everything, and find the rest of this clan." Calum's voice came over the system.

"Body bag?" Devin asked.

"One," Calum said as he motioned for Nox to bring the men through.

"There won't be a trace of them by daylight." Devin's low tone told all those on the comms.

Chapter Twelve

Gia checked the mirror again to make sure there was no movement on the street. There had been very little communication over the radio and the waiting was killing her. She looked up at the roof of the house again, Creed was still sitting there since he'd done a wide sweep around the house. What was happening? She knew it was good that he sat up there, but he was looking in the backyard. There had been nothing on the radio since they said they were taking them back there. Turning, she looked to see Shaelan covering the man's leg with white bandages. The smell of infection filled her nose. How had this man been injured? Had it been while he was abducting one of their own kind? She wanted to ask him, to confirm why she had to do this job, but Shaelan had given him a shot of something when he'd started to come to, and he hadn't moved since.

Bear stood in the open door, the tranq gun aimed at the man. With the first dart and whatever Shaelan had given him, he wouldn't be speaking at all tonight, but Bear wasn't taking any chances.

Evanna had come around and got in the van and handed Shaelan the things she asked for. Gia wanted to ask her who

Minn was, but after the quick explanation from Shaelan before she'd got here, Gia also didn't want to intrude into things she didn't quite understand. Evanna grabbed a bottle of water and got out of the van, she opened it and poured it over her hands, then drank the rest. "I can taste the rot in my mouth." She said quietly.

"I don't know if the leg is saved, but I don't think he's going to be walking very much where he's going." She wiped her hands and surveyed the man once more. "How much time has passed?"

Bear looked at the house and then back, "it hasn't been as long as it feels."

"Coming out through the garage." Deacon's voice came over the radio. "Bring the other vans closer."

Shaelan stepped out of the way when both Evanna and Bear turned, guns raised at the open garage door.

Gia turned back quickly and started the van.

"Send the clean up here, Devin, and get them to go through everything, find the rest of this clan." Calum's voice came over the system. Shaelan turned to look toward the garage.

"Body bag?" Devin asked.

"One," Calum answered.

Gia glanced at Evanna; she didn't seem phased by the information. Her heart was pounding in her chest. Blair had avenged his family; his mate's family and it had been her that had said how it was to be. She licked her lips and looked back at the radio.

"There won't be a trace of them by daylight." Devin's low tone told all those on the comms.

She stared at the radio and then looked toward the garage. Deacon came out of it, he looked the same as he had when he'd gotten out of the van. He lifted his hands and sent Evanna and Bear a look.

They lowered the guns from him.

Lights hitting the mirror had her look in it quickly, the other vans were pulling up.

"Bear, go with Nox and keep an eye on the prisoners."

Bear nodded and jogged down the sidewalk.

Asher came up to Deacon and handed him clothes. Deacon nodded and walked back up the drive and set the clothes behind one of the cars. He looked up and lifted his hand signaling Creed to come down.

Gia's heart beat hard in her chest when Kobie and Blair came into the light. His chest was covered with blood. Shaelan grabbed a handful of bandages and ran over to him.

Blair looked down at her when she reached him.

Gia couldn't hear what he said to her, but she paused and looked at him and then held the bandages out to Kobie. Kobie took them and nodded.

Calum walked by the van; Gia watched in the mirror as he waited until three of the men got in the van behind them. When he lifted the dart gun and shot it several times, she knew he had just knocked out the men they'd found in the house. He spoke to Jesse and then came back toward Shaelan.

"We'll ride with your *patient*." He said the word patient like it tasted bad on his tongue.

Creed came down the drive, pulling his shirt over his head. He looked a little shaky but kept going with long a long stride. Gia didn't even know how that could work—a large man like that becoming a bird? How did that work?

The passenger door opened, and Shaelan climbed in. She looked at Gia, her expression mirroring Gia's thoughts. 'This wasn't at all what either had expected.'

Gia waited until Calum, Creed, and Deacon climbed in. She looked at her phone and then the radio, waiting for the promised information about where they were supposed to be going.

"I'll direct you," Calum said quietly.

She nodded, then watched Deacon close the door before turning in her seat and putting the van in drive, "Do I wait for the others?"

"No, they'll be taking different routes. This one will be going by chopper, the others aren't." His tone didn't leave room for more questions.

"Get out on the interstate and head North."

She glanced in the mirror and met Deacon's look; his expression told her everything was fine. Pulling away from the curb, she kept her eyes straight ahead and focused on driving. Reaching, she pushed the button and put both windows down, hoping the others needed air as much as she did.

Two hours later, Gia put the van in park and turned in her seat to see the somber expressions on her passenger's faces.

"Go grab something to eat, Illias will have the driving schedule ready now," Calum said as he opened the door and got out.

"I'm just going to clean the van up," Shaelan said quietly.

"I'll give you a hand," Gia said as she opened the door.

The males, all three barely acknowledged they'd spoken as they walked by her and went toward the house.

Gia stood there while Webb pulled his van in behind hers. Their expressions echoed the others when they got out. Reaching in, she grabbed her run pack and put it over her head. As long as that phone and envelope were in it, she was keeping them with her at all times.

Going around, she opened the side door and then looked at Shaelan. She offered a small smile. "This one was different." She said quietly.

Gia got in the van and opened the box that had been set in earlier.

Jesse, Evanna, and Asher walked by. Shaelan watched until they went into the house. "If you'd seen what they'd done to some of Kobie's clan members, it would put it into perspective for you."

Gia blew out a breath. "Is Blair okay?"

Shaelan opened a small bag and started picking up soiled bandages. "He doesn't want to heal it," she motioned to her chest, "the claw marks." She stopped and looked at her as Gia took the bag from her hands and held it open. "I imagine he's in there right now rubbing salt on it so he can wear it like a badge to remind him for the rest of his life."

Gia winced. "That was his brother?" She had brothers, and yes, during her life she'd wished them dead, but never literally.

Shaelan nodded, "that's the first time Blair's ever seen him. His mother sent him away to live with Ed's clan when he was two, she saved his life and I'm pretty sure it cost her own to do it."

Gia's heart was racing, "I can't even wrap my head around a shifter helping that man take other shifters."

"And that's why I'm here," Shaelan said quietly. "To end it." Closing her bag, she climbed out and then reached back in and rolled the plastic sheet that covered the floor. Turning, with it bunched in her hands, she stuffed it into the bag Gia held. "Some, whether two-leg or not, are not right in the head, Gia, the sooner you move past the why, the easier it will be."

Gia pulled the bag together and tied it. "I was sheltered from everything all my life, I just want to help."

Shaelan smiled at her, "sometime when we're not on such a hectic schedule we'll sit down, and I can tell you what my life was like."

"Giana."

They both turned to see Deacon standing in the shadow of the house.

"We leave in two hours. I'll drive to the other house if you like, so you can rest." With that, he turned on his heel and headed to the backyard.

At least it hadn't sounded like an order coming from him. Gia blew out a breath. "I guess I better go find out the plan."

Shaelan grinned, "I just go with the flow, let the men stress over the other details." She shrugged, "it's easier that way."

Gia closed the door and smiled at her, "I've never been good at letting men plan my life."

Chapter Thirteen

Picking up the radio, she checked the volume. It was turned up. Of course, she knew this, they'd been on it a few minutes earlier, but her nerves made her look to confirm that. Checking the clock, she turned in her seat and got up. Pulling the med kit out, she set it behind the seat, then looked around. *What else?* Grabbing two blankets, she set them with the med kit.

When Rayne had told them that the people may not be in the best of conditions, there had been an eerie silence. Opening the cooler, she looked to see it was full of drinks. She knew that also because she'd filled it before they left.

Inhaling, she went and sat back in the driver's seat. She needed to be ready when they got the call. Looking at the vehicles spread out down the block, *yep,* they were all there still. Tonight, they had five vans and a larger truck. Deacon had told her the truck was the clean-up, crew. She didn't really know what that was, but last night a body had been part of the deal. One of the vans was going to be for those helping Tomas, but according to Jesse as they chatted on the drive here, Noah had been one of those and now he was helping free others. So how did they know if they were good or bad people?

She was tired but completely wired at the same time. Her mind wouldn't stop—at all. The last two days had been so out of her comfort zone, yet she wouldn't change them if she could. She'd been involved in stopping a group that had been helping the Tomas family for twenty years. *Twenty years.* That was insane. She would have been four when they'd started. How many lives had they ruined in that time? She didn't even want to guess an answer. She had been involved in stopping them, that's what mattered. For the first time in her life, she felt like she had a purpose.

Then there was Deacon, he was a hard one to figure out. He was quiet most of the time but had no problem conversing when the mood struck him. The way he'd stood up for her when Nox had started made her think he was just another male that liked to give orders, but that wasn't the case. He hadn't yet *told* her to do something, not really. I'll drive, turn here or there, didn't really count. She thought of last night on the drive, he may be the only male she'd ever met that didn't jump at the chance to shift and go for a quick run. She frowned and looked out the window, although he'd wanted to stand watch while she did, so maybe his job came before other things.

"Back rooms are clear." York's voice announced.

Snapping her head around, she looked at the radio, waiting. It had felt like an eternity since they'd gone in.

"Two for you, Nox—so far." Calum's tone was as it always was, quiet, calm.

Two? They had two 'prisoners' for Bear and Nox to transport.

"One woman and a boy, cleared," Blair reported. "Completely mobile."

Completely mobile? Their health must be good, or at least injury-free. That was good.

"Transporters, I need names once they reach your vehicles," Devin told them from back at the safe house.

Gia nodded to no one. She looked in the mirror again and didn't care what the others were doing, she was starting the van.

"I have three unconscious that will need a handout, Nox." Deacon's voice broke off her internal chatter.

"Copy." Nox's cold tone made her roll her eyes. Was a

response really required to that?

"Two women, two more boys," Jesse announced to them. "Completely mobile."

"Perimeter secured, bring up the vans." She was pretty sure that was Noah, but honestly hadn't heard him say more than ten words in the days they'd all been working together.

She pulled the van out onto the street and drove quickly to the corner, checking, she saw the others right behind her, all except the big truck. She spotted Noah on the sidewalk looking around him, he motioned for her to pull right into the drive, so she did. Turning it off, she shifted around in her seat and went back and opened the side door.

"Have a blanket ready, Giana."

At Deacon's tone, she grabbed the blanket and jumped out of the van. She anxiously watched the door for him. Blair came out the door first, a small boy and woman with him.

Kobie went running by her, "Alena." When she reached them, the woman almost threw herself in Kobie's arms and hugged her. Kobie released her and bent down to pick up the boy. She said something to Blair. He nodded and turned back toward the house.

"Alena Burch and her nephew Indy, from Kobie's clan," Blair said in a somber tone.

She turned and looked at Creed, then to the radio clipped to his waist. She couldn't help the rush that went through her to know they'd found people lost to Kobie.

Deacon came out the door next, he was carrying a woman. Gia rushed forward, trying to see if she was injured. She looked like she was half unconscious. Her black hair was wet and matted to her face. She was so frail her cheekbones were visible. She reached and put the blanket over her. Her clothes were soaked.

"She was in the tub, fully clothed." He said in a hushed tone.

Gia went ahead of him and had the second blanket in her hand by the time he reached the van. He ducked down and went right in the van with her, setting her carefully into one of the seats. He stayed there, his hands out like he was afraid she was going to fall over.

Climbing in behind him, Gia squeezed by him and tucked the second blanket around her. "You're safe now." She said, unable to hide the emotion in her voice. The woman opened her eyes, then licked her lips like she wanted to speak, but didn't say anything, just closed her eyes and leaned her head back. Gia looked up at Deacon, to find his eyes on her and not the rescued woman. She sucked in a breath to ask if they should call Shaelan here and froze. His scent filled her system, her fox was right there now. *Oh no.* Dropping her chin, she looked back at the woman. She needed to focus right now, and do her job. "What's your name?"

"Terah." Her voice was so weak, Gia barely heard her, "my mother called me Terah Matthews." She licked her lips, "I need to be with water."

Gia moved back and was going to reach for a bottle of water when the woman's words registered in her head. "We'll get you to water." She touched her shoulder, hoping to convey some comfort. "What's your clan?"

She opened her eyes a sliver and looked at her. "I don't know."

Gia had heard there were shifters born in the captivity of the Tomas organization, ones that had never known their own world, but until now she had thought it was an exaggeration. "Don't worry about it, we'll take care of everything."

Deacon moved out of the van and stood beside it. He touched his ear. "Shaelan, we need you up here." He was looking toward the back van.

Gia got out of the van and leaned close to him, she didn't want to talk about the woman *right* in front of her, but also to check what she thought her brain had smelled a minute ago. "Are there water clans?"

Deacon looked down at her, the hard look in his eyes softened, "yeah. I don't know the first thing about them though."

Gia nodded her head slowly, then turned and opened the

passenger door, and grabbed the radio. "Terah Matthews. No clan—, she looked at Deacon as she spoke, "that she's aware of." She cleared the lump out of her throat, "she needs to be near water."

"We'll take her to the campground." That was Rayne's voice on the other end.

"Kynlee Molina and her son, Ari, Lane Cohen, and her son Ronan, all from Kobie's clan." Blair's solemn voice came over the radio.

Deacon turned and jogged to Shaelan, probably telling her that she needed water.

"Is she hydrated?" Shaelan came running over and climbed into the van. "Hi, I'm a healer and going to help you be more comfortable for the trip out of here."

"Am I really free?" Terah asked in a hoarse voice.

"Yes. Yes, you are." Shaelan answered as she opened the bag. "I want to start an IV and get you hydrated. it will help you a great deal until we can get you to water."

The woman nodded and leaned over in the seat, so she was propped in the corner.

Shaelan glanced out at Deacon, "tell Cal, we're riding with you."

Deacon nodded and turned to watch others coming out. "Cal, Shaelan needs to ride with Giana and me."

Calum came out the door, a gun pulled as he escorted two men down the walk. He nodded at Deacon, telling him he heard.

Seeing the gun, Deacon pulled his as well and stood there, blocking the open door of the van and Gia from seeing those they were taking to the van Nox was in.

"Averie Little from Kobie's clan," Noah said over the radio.

Shaelan paused and looked at Gia, her eyes glistened with tears.

Just seeing that made Gia turn away and look at the house as the others came out. Eight. They'd freed eight of their kind from this horrible life. Deacon jerked his head around and looked at her, she didn't need words to know he was wondering if she was okay. She swatted at the tear on her eyelash and nodded her head. She looked over to see Blair and Noah carrying out a man.

"These two are covered in so many scars, it's terrifying." Bear's voice broke through her thoughts as the radio in her hand spoke.

"They all still have to go to the refuge until we know if they can be trusted." Devin's voice came over the radio. "They'll get full medical assessments and anything they need."

She looked over at Deacon.

"They'll be interviewed," he gave her a soft look, "some have been in servitude so long they can't deal with life on the outside."

"I didn't know."

Deacon took a step toward her, then stopped and backed up again. "Noah was one of them, it took him months to be able to function again."

She turned to see Noah carrying another unconscious man, by himself down the drive, the pained look on his face said it all. He was reliving what he'd gone through. Jesse was practically running alongside him. He put his hand on his arm to slow him as they got closer to the van.

"Shaelan is there something in the kit we can put on their necks?" Jesse motioned to the man in Noah's arms. "We can't take the collars off until we are not in a moving vehicle and their necks are raw."

Shaelan put the medical tape on Terah's IV and then turned to look at him. "The ointment won't do much until they're off. Give them all a shot and keep them comfortable until they reach the facility."

Jesse nodded and then turned to run after Noah's long strides.

Gia put her hand over her mouth, not wanting to cry like her heart was telling her she should be.

"Last one coming out," Calum announced.

Gia turned back to look at the house to see Nox and York carrying a large man out. Calum was right behind them.

"Send the clean-up in. There's a lot of paperwork in the one room, save it *all*." Calum growled.

"I'll relay the message. Everyone, get moving. This took too long." Devin's voice was clipped.

"Dev, there's one for the campground, she needs the lake," Calum said in a hushed tone.

"Get her to the chopper." That was the reply.

Gia jumped and went around to the driver's side. She opened it and got in. By the time she had the van started, Calum and Deacon were in with doors closed.

"I know the route for the chopper to the campground," Calum said quietly.

Gia waited for Asher to move his van and then backed out. "Just give me enough warning to turn." She glanced in the mirror to see Terah's eyes were open. Even in the low light of night, she could see they were such a true-blue color that they were almost glowing in the night.

"I want you to try to eat this and then get some rest," Shaelan said quietly. "It's going to be quite a long trip."

Gia kept her eyes on the road. Her heart was racing inside her over what had just happened, but more than that, her animal was now quiet and contemplative. Their mate was sitting beside them. *Their mate.* Could the timing be any worse? She didn't think so. Her animal better behave, she didn't need to be distracted while she was driving. She had to get that poor woman behind her to safety.

Deacon looked over and caught her glancing at him. He took off his hat brushed his hair back and then put it back on the right way. The expression on his face told her so many things. He was happy with how things had gone down and there was pride, and she could only think it was for her somehow. Did he know? Had he figured it out just a few minutes ago when they'd been so close too? Terah said something to Shaelan, and it snapped her attention back to the road. *Worst timing ever.*

Chapter Fourteen

Calum was a smart man, Gia had decided. He hadn't taken them straight to the pickup location but had them circle around through a few areas that had sparse buildings and no traffic. She was taking mental notes the whole time and planning to adopt several of his tactics to figure out if anyone was following them.

"Another twenty minutes and we'll be there," Calum said quietly.

Gia nodded. She checked in the mirror again to see that Terah's skin wasn't as transparent now, but she was a long way from healthy. She didn't understand anything about water clans—at all. Should she research the different clan types? There was no telling who she'd be transporting and knowing how to care for them might be something she should know. As soon as she got a moment, she'd have to message Amari and ask about that.

"Listen up boys and girls." Illias' voice broke the silence in the van. "Safehouse is burned."

A chill went up Gia's spine.

"Five-minute window starts now," Illias told them. "Cal, the wolf and company borrowed your wheels and will see you soon."

She glanced in the mirror to see Calum nod. Her heart felt like it was sitting in the back of her throat. Looking at Deacon, he didn't seem alarmed at all, he turned his hat around backward, then he pulled his clip out of his gun and checked it, then put it back in and rested it on his knee.

"Sister, where are you, I'll meet you?" Nox's voice came over the radio.

Deacon turned in his seat and looked back at Calum.

"Negative." That was Devin, he must have a radio with him. "You are to report to your team leader, big brother."

Deacon sat forward and took the radio off the clip on the dash. "My partner and I will be sticking together." He announced. Then he switched the radio off.

Gia looked at him, she knew her eyes were wide. "He's going to throw a huge tantrum." She whispered.

He shrugged and then smirked at her.

Gia bit her lip and looked in the mirror at Calum. "Can I send a quick message to my brother, Walker, so my mom doesn't worry?"

Calum nodded, "very brief."

"Are they coming after us?" Terah was wide awake now.

"No." Shaelan's tone was soothing, "we'll be fine. This is all just a precaution. You're perfectly safe."

Gia looked to Deacon, his expression said this was not just precautionary. "Can you grab my phone and text Walker for me?"

"Next right," Calum said calmly.

She nodded.

Deacon pulled her phone out of the holder and tapped the screen.

"Just tell him I'm going off the grid for a bit and will text when I'm back." She looked to see him typing, "put love you, bro at the end."

When he was done typing it, he glanced at her.

"That's it." She shrugged, "Walker is my only ally in the family." She added in a hushed voice.

"Sent." He turned the phone over in his hand, "I'm taking the chip out and turning it off."

Gia nodded, "do I look in the envelope now?"

"Wait until you drop us off," Calum said quietly.

"I'm going home." Deacon said and glanced over his shoulder at the large man seated behind him.

"Good choice. Shae and I will go with Devin." Calum answered.

Deacon nodded and turned around. Pulling his phone out of his pocket, he turned it off and then opened the case holding it.

"Take all of the supplies with you." Shaelan's soft voice ended the tense silence. "We'll need it when we meet back up."

Gia nodded, but she was afraid to talk too much. She didn't want the others to know how terrified she was right now.

"Next left and then you'll see the chopper," Calum told her.

Gia looked around, not having the slightest clue where they were now, or even how to find their way to the highway again. "Can we use GPS?"

"Best not to." Calum answered, "Deacon will have maps."

She glanced over to see him nod. "Okay."

"Have a little faith." Deacon said, with a light tone of amusement. "This is what I'm good at."

"Reading a map?" She looked over at him, quickly, not wanting to miss the next turn.

Deacon smirked, "no at disappearing and surviving."

Gia dragged her gaze away from him and turned the next corner. It still felt wrong not to use a signal, but now that Calum had told her that it made sense. She watched in the mirror. No lights or, as Calum had said, interruption of lighting in the area behind them. That man *knew* things.

"How the hell did he beat us here?" Calum sat forward, "he better not have ridden the clutch this time."

Gia smirked, realizing that Calum and the prince had to be friends, for him to sound so annoyed with him.

She slowed the van and was shocked to see a helicopter fifty feet in front of them. Three large, armed men stood beside it.

"Okay, Terah, let's get you over to Rayne. You'll love her." Shaelan told her. "Make sure they have warm blankets, Cal."

Calum jumped out of the van, "move fast and silent." He nodded to Deacon, then turned and jogged toward the chopper.

Gia watched Rayne and Shaelan help Terah walk across the pavement.

"So, where is our ride?"

"Oh," Gia jerked her head back and shifted her run pack around, "let's see." Pulling out the envelope, she opened it and looked at the paper folded inside. "It says. Use the envelope of money in the glove box and go to," she frowned, "I can't read this address." She held it out to Deacon.

He took it and read it, then blew out a breath. "We have to backtrack a lot to get here." He turned to watch Calum helping Shaelan into the chopper. "Start driving, a chopper taking off in the middle of the night is bound to draw some attention."

Gia watched Calum run back toward his car. She put the van into drive, "he's not going with her?"

Deacon chuckled, "and leave his car behind, no. She probably went to keep an eye on Terah."

Gia accelerated and went back out the street they'd come in on, "you'll have to give me the directions."

Chapter Fifteen

Deacon looked over to see Giana was still sleeping. The seat was reclined, she was curled up, with her legs tucked under her. She looked so small, so fragile with her hair spread out on the seat and her face was so peaceful.

He wanted to open the window and take fresh air into his lungs but didn't want her to get cold. There was frost on the ground, that glistened in the moonlight. Her scent was driving him nuts, to constantly be inhaling it with each breath. He'd given up on the mint-scented toothpicks about a hundred kilometers ago, even the strong taste couldn't prevent him from feeling like she was coating his tongue in her essence. Taking off his hat, he dropped it between the seats and rubbed his hand over his hair to prevent it from falling in his eyes. His gaze strayed from the road again to look at her. She was so lovely. It made his chest ache.

His animal wasn't doing much better than Deacon was. Wanting their mate but are not able to do anything about it. More often than not in the last twenty-four hours, his creature had also demanded to be out. When they'd stopped for Giana to go for a quick run, Deacon had paced back and forth beside the vehicle having to fight the whole time to keep him inside and almost under control. He'd told her he didn't want to chance it and should keep watch, and she'd accepted that answer, even offered to do the same when she came back. His excuse then was they should keep moving and she accepted that as well. She didn't remember that there was no way of tracking the vehicle. Illias' team made sure of that. Deacon didn't like lying to her, and it was a struggle to keep his answers or explanations with some sort of truth-ism to them. He glanced at her again—*truthism*, was that even a word? He had no idea, but that didn't mean it wasn't a word, somewhere in the world.

Looking out the window, he glanced around to gauge how much longer until they reached the yard where he left his truck when he was out working. What was she going to think when they ditched this smooth ride for his old truck? She'd probably never ridden in anything other than comfortable vehicles. His truck wasn't bad, in his opinion, a little rough riding, but he'd been working on that when he could, of course, its appearance seemed the perfect image of what he was. The mismatched panels that covered it were different colors as he'd replaced them as he found them, it wasn't pretty to look at, that was for sure. Like him, he supposed, his animal wasn't pretty and sleek either.

He just wanted to get home, go for a long run and kill something. *Home.* That was another problem, his house if you could call it that, wasn't going to be anything she was used to either. The basic cabin, he and Calum had built was small, not meant for comfort, with an enclosed porch larger than the building itself. Deacon spent more time in the porch than in the building, except when the dead of winter was here. There was no power or running water, everything was set up to work off a generator. He rubbed his beard briskly, hoping the old shifter that kept an eye on things had refilled the fuel cans while he was away.

He didn't know much about Beckett, only that he'd fallen off the grid a long time ago and wanted to keep it that way. With Calum's land and cabin twenty minutes from Deacon's smaller plot, the old man watched over both for them. He glanced back at the supplies and decided he'd leave him some of them when he picked up the truck. Juice and some of the snacks were always appreciated.

"How long have I been asleep?"

Her husky tone hit him right in the groin. She stretched and made little noises as she woke slowly. Deacon gripped the steering wheel with white knuckle focus. "A few hours."

Unclipping the seat belt, she leaned over the reclined seat and reached into the cooler.

Deacon looked at her stretched over the seat and sucked in a breath. Forcing his head to look back to where he was driving, he blew it out slowly. Being this tired was not helping him at all.

She sat up and righted the seat as she shook the juice slowly. "They need to equip us with travel coffee makers," she said in a sleepy voice.

"I could use a coffee." He said, even though he'd never been so alert in his life.

"It's so pretty, the frost shining in the moonlight." She said softly. "I'd offer to drive, but I have no idea where we are."

He looked over as she took a long drink, his animal prowled under his skin as he looked at her neck with her head tilted back.

"I hope there's a shower where we're going." She capped the bottle and looked at him.

He cleared his throat, hoping that his voice didn't sound more animal than man when he spoke, his creature was *that* close. "I'll have to start the heater for the water," and pump the water into the tank, he thought, "but it won't take too long." He rarely bothered with hot water when he was there. He'd lived most of his life without the comforts of a home, so it didn't bother him if the water was cold. Maybe he should explain his home before they got there, then the shock might not be as bad. "My place is rough," he glanced over to see her looking at him. "It's not finished by a long shot," he shrugged, "I'm not there much since I joined the team."

"I'm liking living on the road."

She smiled and his animal settled, she was the most beautiful thing he'd ever seen, the moonlight highlighting her face and with her hair down and not hidden under a hat. He cleared his throat and tried to remember what he was going to say. "Everything is run off a generator."

"Really? So, you literally meant you have to heat the water."

He avoided looking at her, not wanting to see how disappointed she was.

"That's pretty ingenious." She set the drink down and reached for her boots, "I wouldn't know the first thing about doing something like that."

Deacon was momentarily stunned by her comment. "Well, to be honest, neither did I, Calum helped me come up with it."

"You're pretty close to him." It wasn't a judgemental tone, just a statement.

"I am. Actually," he looked over at her and smiled, "the land I run on is his property." He shrugged, "when I didn't know anyone or what my life plans were," he looked back to the road, "Cal helped me find that spot and get on my feet." That was a complete understatement. He had literally saved Deacon's life.

"I can't imagine what it's like to make those decisions," she did up the second boot and then shifted in the seat, so she was looking at him, "to not have your life planned for you."

Her tone had a hint of resentment. "You're making your own life, now." He clarified.

"Yes. Yes, I am and it's not going over well with the fam." She smirked, "as you may have noticed with Nox."

Deacon nodded, "I may have detected a bit of that." He looked over at her, then back to the road quickly, "he, uh, isn't going to be working with the team from now on, our team," he looked over to see the surprised look on her face, "Calum and Jesse's call, I guess what you do overrode his necessity."

"Oh," there was no hiding the surprise in her voice, "Jesse said something about it, but I didn't realize his reporting to your team leader meant he was out now. Will another from the incursion team be assigned with us?"

Deacon nodded, "yeah and hopefully they check to make sure there are no brothers or sisters on the team this time."

Giana smiled, "don't misunderstand, I love my brothers, all of them, but my life has been overshadowed by their opinions since as far back as I can remember."

"There's no time for squabbling in the middle of an operation."

"I noticed." She sat forward and stretched her arms out in front of her. "I still can't believe we found eight of our own and freed them." Dropping her arms down she looked back at him, "maybe even more if those men turn out to be okay."

Deacon nodded slowly, "there's nothing better than the rush of seeing the faces of those we get out."

"Is this what you do all the time?"

"More or less." He slowed down so he wouldn't miss the hidden path to the yard. "Guarding officials as well, keeping the peace if there's been an unlawful transition of leadership," he shrugged, "things like that."

"I think it's wonderful. I had no idea what Nox did."

He turned the corner and drove carefully along the rough path, "I was surprised when I found out he was Alpha and on the team."

"He's the second oldest and," she put the window down and inhaled the fresh air, "what was it my mother said, oh, he doesn't do well with diplomacy, so he was allowed to pick his path."

"Diplomacy isn't his strong suit." Deacon grinned.

"He's good at his job though?"

"He is, I trained with him for six months before I was on the team."

"Well, it's good to know he's not an ass all the time, I suppose." She looked out the window. "Are we here?"

Shaking his head, he motioned to the lone shed with the fence around it. "No, this is where Calum and I keep our vehicles when we're home." He motioned around them, "it's a little too rough for Cal's car and I prefer my truck."

"Yes, I don't see his cute little car doing well on the roads here."

Deacon chuckled, "I dare you to tell him his car is cute."

She turned and grinned at him, "I don't think that's necessary."

Chapter Sixteen

He locked the gate and then jumped back into the cab. "It's about a half-hour now." He closed the door, "I made the road into my place really hard to find and navigate." He looked at her, trying to gauge how she felt about the truck. "Sorry about the ride, she's not pretty, but she drives through all seasons without a problem."

She grinned at him, "it reminds me of a truck Walker had, my father hated it, but he was determined to keep it and fix it up." She frowned, "then his responsibilities to the clan overcame his dreams."

"Walker is which brother?"

"The youngest brother, so no need to be trained to lead." She said as she looked out the window.

"He's the one you messaged."

"Yes, he and I are close," she looked over at him, "closer than my parents realize. He's my secret weapon with my dad."

"How's that?" She looked so proud when she spoke of her family. She might hate the restrictions of it, but there was love there.

She shrugged, "he's on my side, but they don't know that." She grinned, "he arranged self-defense lessons for me, while my mother was more focused on prepping me to be a pretty showpiece for the Alpha family.”

He looked her up and down, then turned back to the uneven trail leading them in the roundabout way to his property. “No training required there,” he glanced at her, “the pretty part.”

Her smile was slow, her cheeks flushed enough he could see them in the low light. “Thank you but prim and proper is just not in my genetic makeup, that’s what Walker says.” She smirked, “he says I was meant to kickass and look beautiful while doing it.”

Deacon liked this brother; a lot more than he ever did Nox. “He’s right.”

“What is your family like Deacon?”

He wished now that he had a toothpick already in his mouth, getting one would look like he was stalling, but he needed to clinch one in his teeth. “I, uh,” *great start*, “I don’t think I have any.” That sounded flippant, but it was the truth.

“Oh?”

He chanced a glance at her and was surprised to see such compassion it made him feel like he was in the spotlight. He turned back to watch the rough trail. “Yeah, my mother was from South America.” He couldn’t look at her. It was best that she knew now, it cemented what he already felt was going to be the final reason why they, as mates were never going to happen. “She came over with some clan members,” he shrugged, “but she died when I was a baby, so her friend raised me.” He focused, trying to keep his eyes on the road. “My dad, I sort of remember him, not clearly, he, uh died when I was five, I think.” He nodded.

“I’m so sorry, that you lost them.” She said quietly. “Was your dad from South America too?”

Deacon shook his head. “No, he was from here.”

“Have you never tried to find out if you have family out there?” She was genuinely interested. That was a first, the few in his life he’d told had no interest in details, beyond the fact that he had no clan to claim as his own.

"No. I mean, I may have thought about it once," he did look at her, and it meant a lot that she didn't have a judgemental look on her face, "I'm sure Calum knows, but I've never asked, and he won't share unless I do." He jerked his head back just in time to follow the turn on his trail of deterring obstacles.

"Calum would know?"

He nodded and gripped the steering wheel tighter as the path angled toward the hill. "Yeah, before I could work for the Alliance and be part of the team, he would have had to make sure I didn't come from a long line of anarchists I'd imagine."

"That makes sense." She was quiet for a moment, "my brother, Walker could probably find out if you wanted. He works in the clan offices and has access to a lot." She waved her hand around, "I'm not trying to be intrusive, just if you know your father's last name, you could find out. Who knows you might have family somewhere?"

"It's Parrish. My last name *was* my father's." He wanted to look at her, but unless he stopped the truck, not keeping his eyes on the trail ahead could find them crash into a large tree. "I don't know if I want to. I mean, what would I say, 'hey, I'm your long-lost whatever relation, my father left your clan a long time ago."

"Your father had a clan?" Her tone was quiet, "I thought he was just a—"

"Rogue, like I am?" He finished for her, "no, from what my mother's friend told me he left the clan for my mother, so I'm pretty sure that would make him an outcast, and the welcome I'd receive would be," he chanced a quick look at her, "not very welcoming."

"What type of clan was he from? Some of them are pretty open-minded now."

Deacon hoped if he answered, then she wouldn't start asking about his mother or what he was. "Fox." He said as he turned the last corner in his hideaway trail.

"Oh." Her tone had changed completely. "Yeah, the fox clans here aren't very liberal at all." She touched his arm, "I'm sorry for grilling you for information."

Deacon looked down at her hand, it was warm against his skin. "It's okay, it's just how it is, right?"

She pulled her hand back. "I suppose it is." She leaned forward, placing both hands on the dash. "Oh, Deacon, this is spot is so amazing." She turned and grinned at him, "that," she pointed, "is your house?"

He nodded, not wanting her to be disappointed in it.

"I barely saw it until we were this close." She chuckled, "It blends in with the trees around it." She undid her seat belt like an excited child would be unable to wait.

"I like being able to see, without being seen." He said, not even sure what was going on by her reaction.

"I get it now." She opened the door as he stopped, "disappearing and surviving." She nodded and hopped out of the truck.

Deacon put it in park and got out quickly, he scented the area for anything that didn't belong, there was nothing and no one nearby. "We'll just leave most of the supplies in the truck so we're ready to go if Illias gets in touch with us."

Giana just nodded as she looked all around. "It is so peaceful here."

~

Gia lay there in the dark, she should have been exhausted and fallen to sleep immediately, especially after the hot shower. She was still amazed by the set-up Deacon had here. He'd started the generator—that he had put in some type of enclosure, and once the door shut, she couldn't hear more than a low hum of it working. He'd turned on the pump filled the tank and heated it for her, she had no idea how the water flowed from that tank to the large shower head, but it felt like she was standing in a waterfall when it did. The water was the purest she'd ever smelled, with no chlorine or chemical undertones to it at all. While she'd been in there, he'd lit the stove and warmed up the small space, so it was cozy. He wasn't there when she got out.

She'd found her backpack sitting on the bed and hoped it meant to use the only bed because she was now burrowed under the blankets that smelled of him. Across the room on the small couch, he'd put a sleeping bag, she stared at it in the dark, would he even fit on that? Should she get up and sleep there? If sleep ever found her. It was so silent; she wasn't sure she would be able to.

Her mind kept churning the last few days over and over. Not the first operation, she tried to forget that one. Death wasn't something she ever wanted on her mind. The second one, however, had changed things on so many levels, she still couldn't process all of it. She, the sheltered daughter of an Alpha had been involved in freeing enslaved shifters from the curse of their entire community. She wondered how Terah was and if it would be wrong to make inquiries about her? About the others as well, including the men that have been forced to do the bidding of the maniacal one-form captor.

Flipping to her other side, she stared at the small window, wondering briefly what time it was, the light of dawn wasn't too far off now. Of course, she should be freaking out that the rescue had ended on such a tense note, one with them all having to run and hide, but that didn't bother her. For the few short moments, maybe, but Deacon was so calm through it all that she fed on his emotion and was able to stay calm.

Her heart kicked up a notch every time she thought of him or anything to do with him. In that glorious moment of triumph, she'd felt by doing something to contribute to her world, *finally*, she'd also found her mate. She should be ecstatic, overflowing with joy, as most would be, but she couldn't quite dig deep enough to find that. Growing up, she'd never been one of those gooey-eyed girls that talked about their future mate and how wonderful it would be. No, the last thing she ever wanted then was another male in her life controlling her. She smirked to herself in the low light, or *trying* to control her. A part of her brain, when his scent had drifted to her told her to run, fast and hard, but she wasn't the type to ever run from new emotions, not even if it was for her own good.

Was she happy she'd found her one and only? Honestly, she wasn't sure. His scent on the pillow wasn't helping her seek clarity on the matter right now, yet it made her feel calm. It was all so confusing. He'd intrigued her before she knew and now, intrigue didn't cover it. He was a huge, many-pieced, large, muscular puzzle. When he'd told her of his parents, she'd wept on the inside. He was so strong, so steady. She knew she would be a fragmented version of herself if her existence was the mystery he was. Her family may annoy her to no end but having them was a part of her strength. She smiled, okay, maybe more the driving force behind her determination, but still, she had them.

Flipping onto her back, she looked at the ceiling, she could ask Walker to look into the family name Parrish, if anyone could find the line, it would be him. She bit her lip, that would be intrusive and wrong without his knowledge. He was friends with Calum, if he truly wanted to know he could in a heartbeat, she imagined.

Did he even know they were mates? That popped into her head without warning. He didn't act like he knew. All she'd wanted to do since she found out was look at him and take his scent into herself. Of course, she'd had to ask to go for a run on the trip when all she'd wanted to do was lean over and sniff him like a drug. It was ridiculous, the emotions and urges that went with this mating discovery. He never looked like he wanted to move a little closer or... her eyes popped open; he was always stepping back from her. She turned her head and looked over at the stove, the small window sent flickers of flames throughout the room. Right from that first moment, she'd dragged her fox out of that hole, he'd stepped back. At the first safe house too, and any time since. He had to know.

Blowing out a breath, she tried hard to make her body relax. She was going to give herself a migraine at this rate. Okay, so he knew and hadn't said anything or acted on it. Why? He'd complimented her many times; even thought she was pretty. He'd told her more than once she'd done the right things and stood up for her against Nox. She groaned inside her head, yeah that had to be it right there. Nox. Her charming, overbearing jerk of a brother. Deacon had to work with him and knew there were three more brothers back home. She closed her eyes, she'd run the other way too if she was him.

Rolling over once more, she moved around trying to find a position that would help her relax. She heard the outer door to his huge porch open and slowed her breathing. Faking sleep was something she excelled at, or she'd have been caught a thousand times by her parents growing up. She waited for the door to the cabin to open. Did she dare roll over and look out the window by his small table to see what he was doing? She didn't want to come across as a nag to him. Maybe he just needed some quiet time in his own space, she didn't know how long it had been since he was home and could imagine after a long time away just sitting and doing nothing in the safety of your home was something everyone did upon returning. She closed her eyes and worked to regulate her breathing. Someday, she'd have a home that wasn't filled with too many relatives. A place like this, cozy, safe, and quiet.

Chapter Seventeen

Deacon stood there and looked around in the early morning light. He was stiff and sore from his marathon last night—not to mention getting so little sleep. He'd meant to go in and stretch out on the couch but instead had sat in that chair and stared at her form in his bed, until the birds started their day. Giana was here and in his bed. He clenched his balled-up shirt in his hand. Many fantasies had occurred in the last five years of just that, although in them he wasn't sitting in the porch just looking at her. His groin tightened and his animal hovered at that thought. He looked down at the front of his pants. Now he was going to have to wait for that to go away before he could go for a quick run.

"Is there a method to produce hot coffee in there?"

He flinched as if someone had just stabbed him. He'd been so lost in his own head he hadn't heard the door open. Holding his shirt in front of him, he turned to her. "There can be coffee." He started to grin and the muscles in his face forgot how when he saw her. Her hair was mussed, she had those sleepy, sexy eyes and was wearing nothing but the long shirt she'd slept in.

Gia sent him a soft look. "I might need a pail full to keep

moving today."

He frowned, "you didn't sleep well?" The need in his body settled, and his mate's care took precedence. "The bed isn't the greatest."

"The bed was fine," she brushed the hair back from her face, "my mind wouldn't shut down." She glanced at the ground for a second, "the last few days have been—"

He nodded, "yeah, settling after the adrenalin surges can be hard, you'll get used to it."

She looked up at him, those alluring eyes moving over his body like a caress. "About that coffee, and uh," she blushed, "a bathroom?"

He jerked as if she'd smacked him, then pointed to the small outhouse behind some trees. "Sorry." He frowned, "I have to get a permit for sewers and I, uh..."

Gia shook her head, "it's fine. I'm sure I'll survive it." She offered him a smile, a real one, "I love your little escape here, and having a polished marble bathroom wouldn't quite fit."

She was nothing like he'd imagined. Her being here, he expected disappointment and pouting because it didn't fit her pampered life. It was amazing she liked his place, but also bad, so bad, it made staying away from her harder than ever. "I'll go get that coffee started while you," he motioned in the direction of the building again. Stopping, he nodded like an idiot and walked by her quickly.

That was smooth, like a rockslide. He stared at the percolator and watched the water drip down through the filter at the top. She may find his place quaint and peaceful, but the idiot that owned it was an entirely different matter.

"Deacon, your property exudes calm as I've never felt before."

Calm? The emotions plaguing him right now were anything but calm. He added more water from the kettle. "It just felt right when Calum brought me to look at it." Setting the kettle back on the stove, he turned to her. "I slept here a few nights before he helped me make the arrangements to buy it and they were the best nights of sleep I'd ever had."

"I can see why." She went over and sat on the small couch and pulled her legs up under her. His pulse started beating stronger when she pulled the sleeping bag over and covered up her bare legs

She smiled at him, "this is the first break I've had in a few weeks." She ran her fingers through her hair, moving it off her face. He wanted to go over and touch it. "I was determined to show Amari that I was right for the job."

He cleared his throat, hoping his voice could be found as lust coursed through him. "Amari is a force of her own."

"You know Amari?"

He shrugged, "our paths have crossed a few times when she was transporting or moving people around." He grinned, "she does not like delays.

"I enjoyed getting to know her. She's from an Alpha family too and I wonder if Jesse put us together for that reason."

He dragged his gaze from her mouth and turned to find some cups. He only had two cups, so it wasn't going to be hard, but he couldn't stand there and look at her any longer. "He may have."

"She was great. She's so strong and steady it helped me see that this was what I wanted to do."

He poured a cup and then looked at her, "I don't have milk…"

Gia smirked, "black and mean is how I like it."

He smiled. "That's good because I only know how to make it that way." He took the cup over and set it on the small table beside the couch. Going back, he poured himself one, not that he needed it to feel alert. If he were any more alert, his heart would explode. Taking it, he went over and sat at the table. Looking back over at her, he froze, she sipped the coffee and closed her eyes in a silent appreciation for a moment. He forced air into his lungs. She looked so fucking beautiful even just drinking coffee. Looking down at the mug in his hand, he stared at the black liquid in it. He was in so much trouble right now. Calum better call them back soon, like right now kind of soon.

"Anything from Illias or anyone?"

Deacon jerked his head up to find her sitting there watching him. "No." He shook his head, then had to brush the hair back off his face. "I checked when I got up." Where was his hat? He didn't even know at this point, which was crazy, he always knew where his hat was. Always.

"Are we allowed to reach out and make inquires?"

The way she said it was so proper and cute. "We could, but the problem with that is all my numbers are in my own phone and we can't turn those on." He lifted the cup to his mouth, "there's only one number programmed into my phone, and it says emergency only." He took a sip and burned his tongue.

"Oh." She closed her eyes for a second, then opened them and shook her head. "I only know one number off by heart, and I doubt Walker could be helpful right now."

He noted again that her brother, Walker, she held dearest out of her whole family. "I have a CB to reach Calum, but he's not at his place, so that won't help either."

"I guess we wait then." She looked around. "Do you have anything that resembles food around here?" She smirked, "I'm starving and if you don't the other options are jerky and protein bars or shifting and hunting me down some small critters." Her smile was big when she said that.

Deacon couldn't help smiling when she did. "I have canned and dried goods." He cleared his throat, "I set the traps last night, so we should have some fresh meat later today."

Gia took a sip of her coffee, then set it down. Moving the sleeping bag, she slid her legs out from under her and put her feet on the floor. "Educate me on how to create food with these dried goods."

He was stunned for a moment, that she wasn't disappointed he didn't have fresh ingredients to make for breakfast. He set his cup down and then picked up his shirt. "I can radio Beckett later and meet up with him for some eggs and things later today." He pulled the shirt over his head.

She walked to his cupboards and opened them.

His feet were stuck in place as he looked at the back of her bare legs.

"Who's Beckett?"

He blinked and looked to see her giving him a look over her shoulder. "Uh, he's an old shifter that Cal's known a long time." He shrugged and went over to the cupboard, "he looks after our places and vehicles when we're not around." Taking out the canister of oatmeal, he set it on the counter and looked down at her.

"Can Beckett get us bread, or do you make that yourself?"

He grinned, "I wouldn't have the first clue how to make that." The smile faded from his face as her scent filled his system. She stood there, looking up at him, a soft expression in her eyes and it took every ounce of restraint he had to not lean down and kiss her. "Uh," he turned his head back to the cupboard, "I have dehydrated berries and oatmeal for breakfast."

"That sounds good." She moved away and opened another cupboard and found the two bowls he owned but didn't say a word as she took them out of the cupboard. "What's on the agenda for the rest of the day?" She set them on the counter beside the canisters he was getting out.

"I should get the wood split before winter gets here." He watched her open one of the containers and look in it. His brain reminded him that hot water was required. "Calum and I cut the trees last spring, but I haven't been here much since then." Grabbing the kettle, he turned to see her leaning back against the counter putting a dried berry in her mouth. He licked his lips as he watched her chew it.

"I'd like to help." She made a face, "I've never done that." She pointed at him, "and this year is all about new things for me."

He grinned, "like rescuing shifters."

"Exactly," she grinned, "rescuing shifters, splitting wood, and," she looked around his cabin like she was searching for something, "washing my clothes by hand?"

He laughed, "I can show you how to do that too."

"Perfect because I haven't got a clue." She popped another

berry in her mouth and walked back over to get her coffee. "But first, I should probably put some pants on."

He nodded his head about six times before he spun around to fill the kettle with the pump. *Cal, you need to get in touch soon. Only bad, wonderful fucking things are going to happen here if I'm left alone with her too long.* He clenched his teeth together and tried not to hear her pulling her leggings over those appealing bare legs.

Chapter Eighteen

Taking his shirt off, Deacon wiped the sweat off his face and then tossed it over onto the woodpile. At this rate, he'd have enough split to last for three years. Anxiety and sexual frustration were great motivators. He glanced into the trees behind the house, wondering how long she was going to be gone. His animal was pissed at him right now. Rubbing his hand over his chest, he almost expected to feel marks there. It felt like his creature was gnawing on his ribs right now.

I don't have a choice. That was his mantra for the last two days. He'd convinced Gia and himself that they both couldn't go for a run because someone had to stay with the phones.

Tossing the split wood closer to the pile, he looked at their run packs hanging on the porch door. It was mostly true; they should get a call. It had been almost four days since they'd bailed on the operation and no word yet. Had everyone made it to their destinations safely? Not knowing was driving him crazy. Setting the next log on the block, he looked at the bush again—a lot of things were driving him crazy.

Being with Giana was nothing like he'd imagined. She was not like he'd figured she'd be. Nothing at all like he thought she would be. She'd laughed when she tried her hand at chopping the wood. Many attempts had yielded very few results, but she hadn't stopped and given up. In the end, she had peeled the log into thin strips. He had assured her it would be good for kindling. Then she'd designated herself to pile the split wood. Deacon set another log on the block and looked over at the lopsided stack of wood. It would probably tip if it went much higher.

Bringing the ax down with more force than necessary, the log split, and the ax wedged into the block beneath. Jerking it out again, he glanced at the clothesline where all the bedding hung drying. She'd enjoyed doing the laundry by hand. No one enjoyed doing laundry, more so by hand. Deacon didn't think his clothes had ever been as clean as they were now. He knew his cabin had never been as spotless as it was.

Giana had made him breakfast this morning. Strong coffee, slightly burned eggs, and crispy potatoes. Her skill of cooking on the wood stove wasn't perfect, but it was a damn sight better than his first few attempts had been.

Rolling his shoulders, he went over and got another few logs and tossed them beside the block. Her being here was nothing like he'd imagined. In fact, it was perfect—she was perfect. All of this was making it a thousand times harder for him to stay away from her and not get attached to the idea that *maybe* they could make it work as mates.

Trying to sleep with her so close was slowly chipping away at his sanity, obviously because his brain was on this never-ending loop of rambling shit. Having her this close was slowly killing him. Every breath he took, even outside, brought the sweet fragrance of her into his body. The daytime wasn't as bad as at night when he was lying there in the dark listening to her breathing, knowing she was a few feet from him. He was going to end up an invalid from the lack of blood flow to his brain.

He growled and swung the ax down into the log.

"So that's your secret."

Deacon turned to look at her smiling at him.

"Intimidate the wood so it splits."

Letting the ax drop to the ground, he released the handle

only once he knew it wasn't going to kick back and take a chunk out of his shin. There was no way to not smile back at her. "I was lost in my head."

She nodded, then pulled the hoodie over her head. "I'm going to lose my mind soon if they don't call." She motioned to the phones, "not knowing is hard."

Going over, he picked up his shirt and wiped his damp neck. "I think we would have heard if something else had gone wrong." It was a complete lie, but he couldn't stand her being upset and worrying.

"I suppose." She tucked her hands into the pocket of her hoodie. "I checked the traps, nothing yet."

Did she know that she looked so enticing all the damn time? He cleared his throat and pulled his damp creased shirt over his head. "I can always shift and go round up something to kill later."

She grinned at him, "I couldn't find anything nearby." She toward the bush, "think they know it's Calum's land and avoid it?"

Deacon chuckled, "that wouldn't be surprising." He looked all around them, at anything but her mouth, because he wanted to taste that mouth more than anything he'd ever wanted. "We could always hunt some birds."

"I don't think I'm *that* good of a shot to hit a small bird."

Deacon shrugged, "I could show you." He regretted the words as soon as they'd come out of his mouth. Showing her would involve getting close to her. Getting close to her was all he wanted, and for that reason, it was a bad idea. The first year of knowing he had a mate was easy to resist the need to go find her, he wasn't in any shape to be a partner in any way. Since then, it had become harder to prevent his animal from prevailing and tracking her down. Now she was here. Right here in front of him and it was a constant battle inside, and not just with his creature. "It's uh, a good way to practice moving silently on two feet too."

She went over and grabbed her run pack, "I got really good at sneaking around," she glanced over at him and smirked, "listening in on Alpha business or *man talk*."

That didn't surprise him, her bucking the system she grew up with. "Ever get caught?"

Her eyes widened almost, "a few times. Walker distracted them away from me."

Walker again, that was the member of her family he had to meet and would probably be the one he wanted approval from the most. As soon as the thought went through his head, he spun away from her and looked back at the woodpile. Approval implied there would be a claiming of his mate. He shook his head, trying to clear it. "This woodpile is never-ending." He mumbled in hopes it distracted her from his sudden about-face.

"I can…"

A phone ringing had him turn around quickly.

With an excited look, she opened the pack and pulled out her phone. "Unknown number."

"They'll all be unknown on those phones." He told her and went over closer.

Nodding, she answered it, "hello?" A relieved look appeared on her face. "Jesse, I'm so happy to hear your voice. Hang on I'm going to put you on speaker." She smiled at Deacon and held the phone in front of her.

"You two get where you were going okay?"

Giana nodded again, "yes, no problems. Is everyone else okay?"

"Calum and I are doing check-ins now. You're still with Deacon I take it?"

"We're together." Deacon answered for her.

"Okay, good. So far everyone is fine."

"How are the people we got out? Terah, is she all right now?"

"I was told they're all doing well."

Deacon watched her shoulders relax; she'd been worried about the ones they'd rescued? He felt a quick stab of guilt having not thought of them once. "Do we have confirmation on what happened exactly?" That he had thought about when his head wasn't full of Giana.

"I spoke to Illias a while ago, he's cranky and distracted," there were voices in the background, "even though this is a secured line, I'm not to discuss it, but know that things have been discovered since our last meet."

Deacon frowned at the phone; it was bad enough that they still wouldn't talk about it over a secure line? "Are there new protocols?"

Giana looked up at him, a curious look on her face.

"We're working those out now, trying to get the team back together as soon as possible so we can continue before locations are moved."

Deacon nodded, "Are they still watching the other locations? Have there been any events to suggest that may happen?"

"A few suspicious things have occurred," Jesse said in a level tone.

"Understood." Deacon looked at Giana, she was watching him. He thought of her brother Walker again. "Are we clear to make any calls at this point?"

There was more talking in the background, "Brief ones, no information relayed should be fine. Don't use email or anything else."

"Not a problem." For him it was true, who would he be emailing?

"We spoke to your boss earlier, she suggested we use a system you know, Deacon."

He tilted his head and looked back at the phone. "The one we use to call in?" It was a simple system of number displacement that they used to speak numbers over the comms, in case anyone was listening. The last went first, the first number was at the end and the others were displaced according to the first number called out.

"That's the one," Jesse said. "I don't get it, but Calum thought it was a good way to reach everyone when the rest of this is set up."

"Yeah, it's a secure way."

"Illias will be sending out the information when ready, so keep a piece of paper handy."

Deacon rubbed his hand over his beard. "We can do that."

"Okay, I have one more call to make. We'll talk to you soon."

"Okay, Jesse," Giana said quickly. The line went quiet. She stared at the phone for a second and then looked up at him. "It sounds serious."

Deacon blew out a breath, "yeah, if Illias is irritated, that means someone somewhere failed at their job and information got out."

"What is that system your team uses?" She tucked the phone back into her pack.

Deacon rolled his shoulders, trying to release some of the tension in them, he needed to go for a run soon, "Uh, it's how we send out numbers or addresses over the comms that we don't want others to understand." He waved his hand around, "the numbers are all mixed up, it's confusing to do on the fly, but no one without the key has ever figured it out."

"The key?"

He grabbed his pack, wanting to check the battery level on the phone. Charging them would mean using the lighter in the truck. "A random number will be called out in conversation or a text of just that number." He unzipped it, then looked down at her, "most times before we go out Wynter will give us the number."

"You have to use this number to unscramble information you say while you're out?"

"Something like that."

Giana blew out a breath, "isn't that hard to do while sneaking around doing what you do?"

Deacon smirked at her, and pulled out a small notepad from his pack, "this isn't for writing poetry."

She grinned. "I'll leave the code stuff to you. I can't even do a sudoku puzzle.

She had to stop smiling at him all the time. He cleared his throat, "how's the battery on your phone?"

While she checked it, he paced over to the cabin and looked into the trees. Things were finally happening. That eased the tension riding his spine. Maybe he'd survive this after all. Turning, he watched her put the phone back in her pack. Another day, two tops and they'd be back on the road. He had every confidence in Illias getting this put together fast. *Please be fast.* If he was left here with her much longer, he was going to ruin her life and in turn his own soul. The only reason he'd climbed out of that spiral that his life had sent him on was her. She was the image he carried in his mind. The portrait of beauty and spirit kept the darkness inside him from taking over. If he claimed her, he condemned her to a life as an outcast, as someone others looked at with disdain—and that could never happen.

"Battery is fine." She said from behind him. *Right* behind him, he could taste her on his tongue. He couldn't look at her right now, not when her scent was binding itself to every inch of his body.

"I should go check—make sure we don't have a predator on the land that's scaring the smaller game away."

Chapter Nineteen

Gia watched him walk into the bush. She hadn't thought of the possibility of some animal scaring things off the land when the traps were empty. There was so much to learn about living like this and she wanted to learn. Granted, she'd never be good at chopping wood, but the rest of it intrigued her. She looked at the pile he'd split while she was out running around. The least she could do was pile it. She needed to feel like she was contributing.

Going over, she bent down to fill her arm with the firewood. She'd grown up with thermostats and if you were hungry, just opening the fridge and looking inside. Stacking the wood onto the pile, she looked at his little home. This way was so much more peaceful. Okay, she missed the internet and movies, but things like that were distractions from her life when she wasn't happy.

Picking up more, she checked to see if he was coming back yet, he'd looked tense after talking to Jesse, so a good run was always the best fix for that. *Tense.* She shook her head and then went to pick up more. The last few days would have been the most relaxing in her life if she hadn't been on edge the whole time. Deacon Parrish was her mate and at first, she thought he knew that now she was wondering if that was just his way and not avoidance at all.

On autopilot now, she went over and started a new row of wood in front of the other two. She knew without a doubt that he was hers, her little fox knew that he was and was now her own internal nag as a result.

She paused halfway back to the pile; can someone be your mate but you're not theirs? Was that even possible? Biting her lip, she looked over at her phone and wondered if Walker would know. She laughed out loud because that conversation would go well. He may be her ally in the family, but he was still an older brother.

This was going to drive her mad. She had to do something though. Two days of placing herself close to him for one reason or another wasn't yielding any results. She didn't know what she expected, but him suddenly having an epiphany and saying 'Oh cool, we're mates' was never going to happen. Grabbing more wood, she snarled at it, too bad she wasn't one of those types of females that threw themself at a male. How did they even do that? It was degrading. Worse still what if he denied her? That would be mortifying.

Placing the wood in the new row with a little more oomph than was really necessary, she stopped and looked around. She loved it here. This calm space was what her life had been missing. The mix of adrenalin working with the team and then coming home to this was a perfect combination.

A phone ringing had her spinning around and looking at the run packs. She rushed over and opened hers, it wasn't hers. Biting her lip, she grabbed Deacon's. Missing a call right now wasn't good, it was also why one of them always had to stay with the phones. She took his out and answered it without looking at the screen. "Hello?"

"Gia? It's Calum."

"Hi. Deacon is out trying to figure out why there's no small game in the area." She said it quickly waning to explain why she answered Deacon's phone.

"That's not uncommon at this time of year, they're moving to find shelter before winter."

She hadn't thought of that. There was too much she just didn't know. "Would Deacon know that?"

"I'd imagine he would, we had that issue a few years back. He's probably gone to lay a trail to keep them from leaving the land altogether."

"A trail?"

"Yes, leaving his scent all over the property line. I've used that method a few times."

It was a smart thing she never would have thought of in a million years. "Oh, that's smart."

"I was just checking in with him to see how he's doing."

"Quiet and broody." She said out loud before she thought it through.

Calum chuckled, "that sounds about normal. How are you doing?"

"I'm good. I love it here. It's going to be sad when I have to go back to my other life."

"I see."

She frowned, that was an odd answer. "Deacon seems really agitated today, any idea when we're going to be called back? I think he's missing his job."

Calum chuckled again, "I'm sure that's it. We're hoping we'll have things put together in the next day or so."

Gia looked around. Another day here, then what? "How is Terah doing? You're there where she is right?"

"Physically she's recovering. It's going to be a long while before she settles in though."

"She's never been anywhere else, has she?"

"No." His tone was colder, "she was born into servitude."

Gia's heart ached for her. "I'm so glad we found her."

"There will be more like her. I will let you go. Tell Deacon I called and for him to stop running."

She frowned. "Okay." Did she ask what that meant? It was probably something that only the two of them would understand.

"Keep the phones handy, Gia. Bye."

The line went quiet. She looked at it. That was interesting.

Putting it back in his pack, she zipped it back up.

Turning around, she surveyed how much wood was left. She should finish that and then check to see if the sheets were dry.

Washing by hand was more enjoyable than she imagined. It wasn't thrilling or anything, but there was something peaceful and simplistic about it.

Turning full circle, she looked around the area. Was it the man, her mate that was making her discover this side she didn't know she had or was it this slice of serenity where he lived? She was sure, suspected it was a combination of the two.

Going back over to the woodpile, she knelt. Her entire life had been on public display, and she'd hated it. Maybe all she needed were callouses, blisters and no electricity to feel peace. Filling her arm with the wood, she stood up. Of course, if she could figure out how to get her mate to *be* her mate, things would settle inside her and she'd feel less like a ping pong ball with tension, highs, and lows of emotion and her animal irritating her like no one ever had before.

Chapter Twenty

Deacon paused to scent the air. The animals hadn't left the land, just moved to the areas with the denser growth to shelter from the winter. He'd have to move the traps to different locations to try to catch them in the new paths they'd use.

His animal was not happy today, even being out. He'd had to reign him in about ten times so far when he'd picked up Giana's foxes' scent. He wanted to follow it back to her and that, Deacon had adamantly reminded him was not going to happen.

He turned and started an easy run back toward his home. With his long legs, even a slow run was too fast. Every second he was near her it became harder to resist touching her, kissing her...

He growled low, thoughts like that were not helping.

For the past day and a half Gia's fox, even without shifting had been giving off pheromones like crazy. It was like a drug to his animal—he couldn't get enough of it. Unfortunately, it also meant that Gia knew they were mates. So far, she hadn't brought it up or pushed trying to get closer to him. Which was good. He turned to go the longer route. If it was so good, why was it annoying the hell out of him more? He didn't want her to be mated to him. Without warning, his animal stopped suddenly, it took a moment for Deacon to realize that despite getting exercise, his thoughts were being shared with him. The creature wasn't happy with the idea that Deacon didn't want to be mated to Gia.

Snarling at nothing, he forced him to start moving again. Of course, Deacon *wanted* her, but sometimes what you wanted and what was able to be were two different things.

He needed to reach out to Calum, and get things going again soon. Lasting years without tracking her down he could do just fine, but when she was ten feet from him—he wasn't going to last much longer.

Forcing his mind to pay attention to what was around him, he checked the trees to see if there were any birds in the area. There was a chill in the air today, with that smell of winter and what they didn't need was a big storm to roll in and to get stuck here. It had happened only once before. Getting snowed in with Gia was not an option, he'd push the truck through it if he had to.

When he'd stalled as long as he could, he turned to go back. There was enough wood left to split that it would occupy and distract him for the rest of the day, hopefully.

When he heard a screech, he cleared the last hill that led down to his cabin. It was Giana. Something was wrong, she was frightened. Pouring on the speed, he darted around trees in his path. He should shift. The thought was replaced with panic, but if the threat was serious, what was he going to do buck ass naked? There was no choice, he had to stay in this form, whether man or beast was the cause of her fear, he could deal with them in this form, at least until he got to his guns.

As he reached the house, he slowed down so he could assess what was happening before running into whatever situation was on the other side of it.

"I am not scared of you," Giana said with a venomous tone. "Just stay away from me and get out of here."

Deacon had to keep a lid on his animal, it wanted to rush in and save their mate. He glanced at the truck, getting there and getting a gun was going to take some fast moves. He heard the door of the porch close. They were inside his home.

Giana screeched again and he bolted around the house, then came to a sliding stop as she spun around inside the porch swinging her hoodie in the air. *What the hell.* He stood there as she opened the door held it with her foot and swatted the air with her shirt again. A bat came out the door and circled up toward the trees.

A bat. She was screeching over a bat, no intruders.

"Get out of here, you're not welcome here." She called to it, then huffed out a breath and stood there in the open door. "Snakes and frogs, even bugs I can do, but I can not do flying rodents." She was brushing at her hair with her hand.

If it were possible to laugh while in animal form, he would have. She had no problem with any part of his home and the situation but was so indignant over the bat that it struck him funny.

"Oh no, you don't." She ducked down as the bat swooped in her direction. It flew right back into the porch. "Dammit." She growled and then stepped out of the door and closed it, standing on the outside. "Now what?" Hands-on hips she turned and looked around then froze.

Deacon realized she'd spotted him. He was so caught up in watching her that, he forgot what form he was in.

"What...Deacon?"

Shit. Shit. Shit. Too late now. This would cement things for her with this mating issue. Still, he didn't think he could see fear or abhorrence on her face when it was directed at him.

"It *is* you."

He stared at the ground and watched her feet bring her closer. He couldn't see that look on her face. He wouldn't survive it.

"Look at you."

That part was different, it was usually what are you? Yeah, he needed to go shift back and face the questions in a form he could answer with.

"You're beautiful." She said breathlessly.

Huh—what? He jerked his head up to see she was only a few

feet from him.

She rolled her eyes, "not beautiful like pretty, more of an amazing kind of beautiful." She moved closer.

His animal chose now to assert his control and Deacon couldn't have gotten his feet to move for anything.

"You take after your mother's clan, right?" She smiled at him, a soft look in her eyes, "I just assumed you were a fox, but you are so much more than that." She came right over to him and ran her hand softly down the dark red mane that ran from the back of his head to behind his front legs. "So soft." She put her other hand on him and rubbed along his shoulder to his chest, "and you're so tall."

Deacon couldn't move, he was barely able to breathe. No one had ever touched him in this form, in fact, they usually ran from him.

She leaned down, "I can't believe your eyes don't change, the color," she clarified, "you're amazing," she whispered.

He didn't know if it was him or his creatures doing, but he lifted his chin and licked along her throat. When the taste of her hit his tongue, he reared back from her and took off in the direction of his clothes. That was insane. What had just happened? And why—what in hell had possessed him to lick her?

Jamming his hat on his head, he ducked under the tree and walked into the clearing in front of the cabin. She stood there watching him as he did. His heart felt like it was stuck in his throat, he could barely bring oxygen into his lungs.

She put her hands on her hips and gave him a hard look.

Here it comes, he thought.

"I am *so* jealous." She said, then motioned to her leg, "I would kill for legs that long in any form."

He stopped walking and looked at her as she smiled.

"Seriously Deacon, what clan was your mother from? I mean I know it has to be one in South America because I've never seen someone like you before."

"Ah, Calum said she was a maned wolf." He mumbled it,

still not believing she wasn't freaking out right now. He'd looked it up online after Calum had told him. Neither fox nor wolf. That part stuck out more than the rest of the information. It fit though, he was essentially a species that was neither one nor the other, but something in between.

"Are there more here? In Canada?"

He jammed his hands into his pockets. "I don't know."

"Is the coloring from your dad? The dark red, I'd know fox coloring anywhere."

"I'm not sure." He watched her from beneath the peak of his hat, unsure about making eye contact with her.

"Wait," she started walking toward him, "what's wrong?" She frowned but kept coming closer. When she was close enough, he could feel the heat from her body, she looked up at him. "Is that why you won't run with me?" Her grey eyes held his prisoner. She was so close he could clearly see the gold fleck in them, they made her eyes look like they sparkled. "I mean, you could no doubt outrun me with those legs, but still company is more fun sometimes."

He shrugged one shoulder, "we do need to stay near the phones."

"We could take the phones with us, and you know it."

Now she had that indignant tone, and it was directed at him. "I just, I'm used to running alone." Or with Calum, but he didn't add that part.

"You should share that part of yourself more, it's pretty amazing. I'm sure it's common on another continent, but here it isn't."

All he could manage was another slight shrug.

She searched his face, and he couldn't decipher what the expression was. Before he could figure it out, she put her palm against his chest, the heat of it felt like it was branding him through his t-shirt. Her eyes locked on his as she stretched up and put her hand behind his head, applying pressure so he would lean down toward her. He could feel her breath against his mouth and was mesmerized by the closeness, shocked she was touching him, even now that she knew what he was.

When her soft mouth touched him, he jerked his hands out of his pockets and put them on her hips. He intended to push her away from him, but instead, he was pulling her closer until their bodies were so close air couldn't fit between them.

Deacon wanted to taste her. Needed to. Turning his head, he kissed her, taking his time, letting their breaths mix and become one. Her mouth was so soft, so warm. Putting his hand against the back of her head, he almost moaned against her lips, her hair was like touching silk.

She opened her mouth to him and he didn't hesitate to insert his tongue inside. The flavor of her was so much stronger than the scent that had been haunting him. She was so potent he felt drunk from it.

Giana moaned softly and pressed her body into him. Just that sound had him harden against her. Bending his knees, he wrapped his arm around her and lifted her up against him. Straightening his legs again, he deepened the kiss. It felt so good having her touch him, feeling her soft curves pressed into him. His hat was gone as she gripped his head and kissed him with such passion that he was sure there would be smoke rising from them.

He wanted to lay her down, right here on the ground and strip the clothes from her and taste every inch of her body. He'd imagined it a million times. How she would taste and feel, what it would feel like to have her beneath him, submitting—

Jerking his head back, he fought for air as he looked at her. He could feel her breasts moving against his chest as she tried to catch her breath. "We can't," he shook his head, "this can't happen." He lowered her to the ground and released her.

"What do you mean?" She kept her hands on his chest and looked up at him. Her eyes were heavy with need, her lips were red from his kiss.

"You're an Alpha, I'm not."

"What?" She blinked, "what does that have to do with anything?"

"It's just how it is, Giana. You're from an Alpha family—a pure bloodline and I'm a mutt." He stepped back before he changed his mind and grabbed her again. He took another step to add more space. "I need to go move the traps." He walked by her and grabbed his run pack this time.

"Calum called while you were out. He said to stop running." She called after him.

He spun back to her. "Did he say anything else?"

Crossing her arms over her waist, she shook her head, "something about the animals moving for winter." Dropping her arms, she gave him a hard look. "That's all you have to say about this. That I'm from an Alpha's bloodline?"

Putting the pack over his head he realized he didn't have his hat on. He started back.

Giana dipped down and picked up his hat. "Do you think that matters to me?"

He stopped in front of her and held out his hand for his hat. "It should."

She tossed his hat at his chest. "It doesn't."

Putting it on his head, he started walking, "I'll be back in a while. You should call your brother and check in with him." He kept going.

"You know we're mates." She called to him louder than necessary.

Deacon stopped and looked at the ground, trying to decide if he should lie to her or not. Lifting his head, he turned to face her.

"How long have you known?" Her arms were crossed over her chest this time. Her temper was stirring, he could see it on her face.

"Since the first time, I sat down beside you at that clan gathering." It was out of his mouth before he knew what he was saying. *Truth it is.*

"Seriously? You've known that long and didn't think to share that information with me?"

Lifting his hands, he held them out, "were you ready to be all mated up at nineteen?"

"No, but that's not the point." She made no move toward him.

"The point, Giana, is your family, your clan would never let their princess be mated to a mutt like me, and I don't blame them." The fact they were standing this far apart and growling back and forth would no doubt be amusing later, much later, after his heart healed again—if it did.

"If you know me at all, you know what they think means *nothing* to me." She stomped a few feet toward him and then stopped and waved her hands around. "I didn't ask to have Alpha blood, I didn't ask for the life I was born into, Deacon, you should understand that."

He could hear that he'd hurt her and it was going to be his own private hell. "I do, but regardless of how you think you'd feel I'm not taking a chance of ruining your life." His animal was going ballistic inside him right now, he couldn't deal with her anger and a pissed-off creature at the same time. "I'll be back shortly." He started walking before he could change his mind.

"And what about your flying rodent pet? What am I supposed to do about *that?*" Her anger was very clear now.

Deacon lifted his hands but kept walking. "I'll deal with it when I get back."

"Thanks for *nothing!*" She screamed at him.

Chapter Twenty-One

Gia looked over at the porch. She should probably go back in and clean that up. Two hours had passed, and Deacon still hadn't come back. She squeezed her eyes tight for a second, still so annoyed with him she couldn't breathe. He knew. He'd known for a long time and had done nothing about it. She'd already conceded that if he had made a move or told her five years ago, she would have laughed in his face and told him to get stuffed.

The idea of setting his fur coat on fire with a propane torch came to mind about an hour ago as well. She'd gotten over that one, mostly.

Now she sat on the unsplit logs and stared at the bush where he'd gone in. Twenty times she'd started after him and changed her mind every time. One thing that was consistent with her is she always went with her first thought with everything. This time the first one was to let him walk it off and then they'd talk. Okay, the full version of that had been let him walk off a cliff, but close enough. Chasing after him was something she wasn't going to do.

Turning, she glared at the porch. The good news was she'd dealt with the bat on her own. The bad news was Deacon's porched hadn't faired very well. She'd tried to catch it with a towel, and a pot neither worked. When it had done a fly-by and touched her hair again, she'd come outside to regroup. A short while later it was on the porch dead. Chopped in half, and the ax was still stuck in the porch floor—one of his wooden deck chairs was missing an arm. But she *had* dealt with it by herself.

Blowing out a breath, she stood up and looked at the sky, like answers were going to be there. Groaning, she went over and looked it the window at the mess she'd made. She did not want to touch that and had already tried to get the ax free. Apparently, she had swung with a lot of force, because it was in there good. Maybe a walk to settle down and then deal with it.

Going around the side of the house, she spotted a fishing pole hanging on the house. Fishing, she could do that. She went over and stretched to get it off the wall. It was longer than she was tall, but she did know how to use one of these. There was just a bare hook and float, so she'd have to get creative for bait, but she was going fishing. Anything was better than sitting here staring at the trees waiting for her *mate* to come back so she could finish yelling at him. Ten steps later, she sighed again and turned around to grab her pack. *Keep the phone close.*

It had taken her a lot longer to find the river than she would have liked. She was going to blame that on Deacon, all she could taste was him and it had affected her scenting the direction of the water. She grinned at the fish flopping on the grass beside her and decided one more and that would make a good dinner. Having skipped lunch because she was too angry to eat, she needed to have dinner.

Opening her pack, she pulled out the phone. Jesse had said a call was okay. Brief and no information, she could do that. How short was *brief?* She didn't know but if she didn't talk to someone soon, her head was going to explode from all the thoughts whirling around in it.

Checking the tension on the line, she decided it could float around for a few minutes while she dialed her brother's number. She didn't even know what she planned on telling him, but just hearing his voice would be good enough.

"Hello?"

"Hi, it's me."

"Gia. I had no idea who could be calling me with an unknown number." He sounded relieved.

"Yeah, long story. I'll tell you another time."

"What the hell is going on? I get that text from you, then you don't answer, all hell has broken out at the clan offices and now you're on some convert phone?"

Taking off her hat, she dropped it beside her and ran her hand through her hair. "I can't say."

"I'm not allowed to use our office computers temporarily." She heard a door. "Hang on let me get out of the house."

She watched the float on the water as it moved with the slight ripples.

"Okay, I'm back. Shit is intense around here." He sounded all worked up. Which was the opposite of what she needed right now.

"I know."

"Nox called Dad and I don't know what the hell he said, but Dad was in a mood after the call."

Gia closed her eyes, "yeah we were on the same team, and he was being," she opened them and smirked, "Nox, so he's off the team now."

"And they kept you over him? Damn. That explains Dad's mood. So where are you?"

"I can't say."

Walker laughed, "you can't tell me anything or where you are—so why did you call?"

"I thought I'd better let you know I'm okay."

There was a long pause, "you don't sound okay, what gives?"

She blew out a breath, trying to sort out in her head what to say.

"Sister, my heart, talk to me."

There was the tone she needed, that one that he had used

every time she needed him to. The one where she could tell him anything and he would listen and help her fix it. "My partner on the team is from Nox's and," she winced, "he's my mate." She let go of the rod and waved her hand toward the sky, "and he's known for years. *Years* Walker and I didn't— and he didn't do anything about it." She snorted, "and now he says we can't because I have *Alpha blood* and he's a mutt." She rolled her eyes, "I don't even know what that is. Is it a real term or what? I don't know." She glared at the water, "I don't know where he is right now, he went to move the traps but didn't come back, I killed a bat with an ax and now I'm fishing." She sighed.

"Uh, Jesus, I haven't heard you speed talk like that in years." He cleared his throat, "you found your mate?"

She nodded and then remembered he couldn't see her. "Yes."

"What do you mean he says you can't be mated because of your Alpha bloodline?"

"That's what he said." She lifted her hand, then dropped it again.

She heard him blow out a breath and could picture him rubbing his hand over his brow like he did when he was thinking. "What clan is he from? Is he one of ours? I don't follow who's on Nox's team."

"He's not from ours." She could see Deacon standing there as he had earlier in his animal's form. "His mother was from South America…"

"Jesus, I can barely remember clans from *here*."

"His father was from here. His last name is Parrish." Surely talking about this wasn't giving away too much, what would anyone else do with this information.

"Parrish." He blew out a short breath, "if I had use of my computer at the office I could look, *but* that won't happen."

She bit her lip. "He's not a fox, Walker." She winced, "his father was."

"Ho-ly shit, Giana." He made another long-drawn-out breath, "oh, sister, you are going to give me grey fucking hair one day."

"Hey, I don't get to choose my mate, it just is." She reminded him.

"Okay. Okay, I know, but just once if you could do something normal and expected, that would be something, huh?" Another breath, "So what clan was his mother?"

"Maned Wolf." She whispered.

"I don't even—wait, yes I do." He made some sort of sound, and she had no idea what it meant. "It was on a list, I don't, *fuck*—remember where I saw it, but, sis, his kind is almost gone from this world."

Gia sat straighter, "what does that mean?"

"*That* is your hail-fucking-Mary, sister my heart. It's rare for mixing of the clans to happen and it can *only* happen if there is a true mating," he mumbled something she couldn't understand, "it's in some by-law for our people or something, *but* with him being a rarity, it might," he snorted, "it's highly unlikely though, it might not make Dad's face go purple where those veins in his forehead take on a life of their own—"

Eyes wide now, she looked across the river. "I don't care what Dad thinks about all of this."

Walker laughed, "you never have."

She realized how long they'd been talking. "Shit, Walker, I have to go. We were told brief calls only on these phones."

"Uh, okay. Look drop me a text when you can, and let me know you're well. If they let me back on the computers, I'll look shit up for you."

Gia nodded. "Okay."

"Hey." Walker's tone had softened, "look, if you're happy, don't let anyone fuck it up, you got it?"

She smiled, her eyes watering. "Got it. Love you, Bro."

"Be safe." He hung up.

Gia looked at the fish beside her, "you hear that, don't let anyone fuck it up." She smirked, "even my unwilling mate." The fishing rod started to slide off her leg. She grabbed it before she lost the rod and the fish.

Chapter Twenty-Two

Deacon had no idea how long he'd sat against the tree and looked down over the valley. He'd moved the traps hours ago and then just started wandering with no destination in mind. He couldn't shift, there was no way he could control his animal right now. His animal only wanted one thing and she was petite, with silky red hair and freckles sprinkled across her nose. She also tasted better than Deacon could have ever dreamed she did. Licking his lips, he confirmed he could still taste her. He looked beside him and wondered if he rubbed dirt on his tongue would her taste last through that?

Kissing her had been the most idiotic thing he'd done in his life. He frowned, okay, in his life since becoming an adult, there were a few sketchy moments when he was a teen. Not only had he kissed her and tried to consume her for a few short moments, but he'd also then confessed he'd known about their status to each other and that he had no plans to take it further.

He should have hidden the ax and all the guns before he'd walked away. How long did it take for women to calm down? He had no idea. The women from the group he grew up around were fiery-tempered, surely all females weren't like that. Of course, the only female he'd been around in the last few years was his team leader, Wynter and she checked exactly zero boxes on the female checklist, so that wasn't helpful at all. He rolled his eyes, that wasn't right, she was definitely female, but her mannerism was, well, he had no idea what, she scared the hell out of him and any other man near her.

He looked at his pack and wished he had Calum's number. Cal always had answers to problems. Sometimes his answers were like puzzles, but there was a solution somewhere in it, and right now even a puzzle to take his mind off how fucked up he'd left things with Gia would be good. The phone in his pack rang and he dove on to get it. Calum always had perfect timing, it had to be him.

"Hello."

"Deacon."

He sat forward, not Calum but Wynter. "Yeah."

"Could shit get any more fucked up?"

He nodded, though doubted they were thinking about the same thing.

"Calum just told me everyone made it out without issues, but let me just say I am getting so sick of this shit, and if I find…"

"Boss?"

"Nothing. Just pissed off. Okay, so the reason I was talking to Jesse is Nox is out." She chortled, "what are the odds that I'd pick one of mine that was related to one of his." She laughed. "Siblings should *never* work together. I should know, if I had to work with my sister, I'd probably slice her into pieces."

Deacon didn't know what to say to that.

"I'm trying to decide who to send back. Do you have any input?"

Pulling his leg up, he leaned on his knee. "Me?"

"No, the other Deacon I'm talking to. I know you guys get antsy when you get downtime, but focus. I don't want to be shuffling my team around every other week. It's a pain in the ass."

"I guess any of the others on the team are fine."

"You guess? Did I catch you having a nap? You're usually a lot more assertive with your words."

Deacon sighed, "Sorry, my head is a mess right now." He winced as soon as he said it. Of all the people to say that to, Wynter was probably the one you'd never want to.

"That is not what I want to hear. I want to hear, I'm solid boss, I'm good to go, boss—what the hell is going on?" He heard muffled voices and wondered who she was talking to. "Who are you partnered with? They told me somewhere…"

"Giana Marin."

She snorted, "Nox's sister. Is she as kiss ass as her brother? Don't get me wrong he's solid when he's on point, but off-mission he's annoying as shit."

Getting up, he leaned his forehead against the tree, stick with answering what she asks. "She is definitely not a kiss ass, boss, exact opposite."

"Ha. I like her already. You two should get along great then, what's the problem."

The facts. The facts. He chanted in his head. "We, uh, get along."

"Shit on a stick, Deacon you're not sleeping with her, are you?" She whistled out a breath, "I'm not your mama, I don't care who you stick it in, but you have to work together…"

"She's my mate." He blurted out when he felt he should defend Gia.

"Aw, ain't that nice." The sarcasm was heavy. "So, you're all mated up and shit, great, there shouldn't be a problem then."

Deacon blew out a breath, not even knowing how to or what to say to her. This was Wynter, she was as compassionate as a rattler.

"You keep sighing like that, kid and I'm going to think you're blowing in my ear—and I don't like you *that* much." She chuckled, "should I be checking clans from the team and try to match up some more members for Jesse? Because you know I'm all about that happily ever after shit."

Deacon shook his head, "no, boss. Whoever you pick

should be just fine to work with the team."

"Oh well then." She mumbled something, "just to be on the safe side I'm going to send Konner, there are so few of his left the chances of him finding his sweetheart is next to fucking never, *and* you would have to be working underwater for that to happen."

Deacon nodded, "Sounds good, boss."

"I'm not a complete heartless bitch, so I'm going to ask you once, kid, do you want to stay on the team with your *fated* mate? Because you need to spell it out for me, some guys just can't handle working with their women, so if you're one of those tell me now."

Deacon blew out a breath again, then cringed because he knew she'd hear. This was his way to end any possibility with Giana. If he didn't have to see her all the time, he wouldn't end up ruining her life. It was the perfect solution. The only flaw with that plan was now that he'd seen her again five years later, the thought of not seeing her made him want to kill—everything.

"Are you still there?"

"Yeah." He took a deep breath to tell her he wanted off the team. "I'm okay staying on the team." Came out of his mouth instead.

"You are so full of shit. It's a good thing I like you." She chortled. "Get it sorted out with her, kid, I don't need reports of you fucking up and mis stepping—*again*."

"Okay, boss."

"We're solid?"

"Solid." He lied to her again.

"Go spray your territory or something." She hung up.

Deacon dropped to his knees and looked down at the phone. What the hell happened? The connection from his brain to his mouth was broken. *Perfect.* He needed that like he needed to shoot his own foot. He winced, no, he'd done that when trying to learn how to use a gun five years ago. *Shit. Fuck.*

Lifting his head, he looked around. By the time he got back, it was going to be dark. If he was lucky, Gia would not be waiting for him with a gun in her hand. Filing the paperwork that he was shot by his mate with his own sidearm would look really bad in this file. Of course, any superiors reading it would laugh their assess off—and then he'd be a joke again.

The cabin was almost dark. He could see the glow from the stove, but no other lamps were lit. Opening the porch as quietly as he could, he kept his eyes on the door, waiting for it to fly open and a small angry woman to be waiting for him. When that didn't happen, he went inside almost in slow motion so he wouldn't wake her. He paused and looked across the darkened room to see her form in his bed. He slowed his breathing and listened; she was sleeping. Not fake sleeping either, she was out like a light. He turned to go back out and saw the plate on the table. Going over he leaned down and inhaled. Fish? She'd made fish for dinner? He shook his head, no, she caught *and* made fish for dinner. *Shit.* Picking up the plate, he moved back toward the door, there was no way he was adding more insult to pushing her away when she'd caught and cooked him dinner. He was eating every bit of it.

Stepping back into the porch, he closed the door in slow motion. Pulling the lighter out of his pocket, he turned to light the candle on the table. Reaching for it, he realized the table wasn't where it should be. Did she rearrange the porch? Flicking the lighter, he held it up. The porch was a write-off. He turned, searching for the candle, and found it laying on the floor. Setting the plate on the chair, he bent down and picked it up. What was that smell? Lighting it, he held it over where the table should be. The table was tipped over, and between it and the other chair was his ax sticking out of the wood floor.

Getting up, he moved over and looked at the ax. He couldn't help the smirk on his face. She'd chopped the bat in half—and left it there with the ax sticking out of the floor. He lifted the candle and moved it around. One arm was split off his chair. What kind of person chased a bat around with an ax?

He stood up and held his hand against his forehead. He was so grateful he took his time coming back, at least long enough for her to get it out of her system. With an ax. Turning, he looked at the door, then shook his head again. She was something.

Lifting the plate, he sat down in the chair and set the candle on the floor. He was eating what she'd made and then cleaning this up—then locking his ax in the small shed outside. He nodded as he put the first bite in his mouth, never letting her use the ax again. The fish was good. *Damn. I'm an idiot. What the hell am I doing? Wynter gave me an out and instead I just volunteered for torture for the rest of my life.* He glanced at the bat, "you got off lucky, bud."

Chapter Twenty-Three

Gia stood beside the stove, a blanket wrapped around her, trying to warm up. If she was honest, there was one thing she did miss, indoor plumbing. Getting up and going outside when it was still dark out and the air was chilled sucked. She didn't want to think about what it would be like in the winter.

The stove had been refilled, so Deacon couldn't have been back that long. She stood there looking at him in the dark. He'd even cleaned up the warzone in his porch.

What to do about you... She listened to his breathing; he was sleeping. She thought about what Walker had told her, not that it made any difference to her if Deacon was one of so few. She'd been intrigued by him before she even realized what he was to her. He was kind to her and had yet to tell her what to do. It may seem petty, but that was important to her, a male that would let her be who she wanted and not what she was expected to be. She didn't pick the family she was born into, but she could control her own life direction.

Releasing her bottom lip, before she bit right through it, she relaxed her grip on the blanket now that she was warmer again. It's a matter of choice, she thought, I could choose to follow what my parents want or go against them. She grinned, where she stood right now made it clear she wasn't doing what her parents wanted.

Looking around the cabin, she tried to picture if this was home, all the time. She could live with that, of course, indoor plumbing would have to happen. Other than that, there was nothing she would change.

Walker's voice echoed in her head *if you're happy don't let anyone fuck it up.* Tilting her head, she looked at Deacon. He mumbled something and she froze, thinking he was awake. When he shifted and said nothing more, she realized he was sleeping. Picking up the blanket so it wouldn't get caught on anything she went over and stood at the end of the couch. He looked like he was sleeping in a chair, he was too big for it. His legs hung over the arm of it, his shoulders were as wide as it. He tried shifting again and the sleeping bag laying over him slid to the floor.

Gia sucked in a breath and held it as she let her gaze caress his naked chest and abdomen. She had a thing for muscles— arms, legs, waist, it didn't matter what part of the body, she just found the sculpted form of a muscle sexy. Deacon Parrish had nothing but muscle covering his tall body. Having tried her hand at chopping wood, it wasn't hard to figure out how he got to be that way.

Moving closer, she intended to pick up the sleeping bag and put it back over him, but as she bent down to get it, she inhaled his scent, and a shiver of awareness went through her. How did he expect to work together and ignore the fact that their animals were mates? Kneeling on the material she'd meant to pick up, she looked at his face. So relaxed in sleep. No trace of that crease across his brow that marred his good-looking face. Biting her lip, she stared at his beard. When they'd kissed, she found out it was course, such a contrast to his soft lips. She hadn't minded it at all and it gave him a look of a ruggedness, that she couldn't deny was very drawing. He sighed in his sleep, shifting more onto his back and she watched his chest settle back in the rhythm of sleep.

She should be annoyed with him for sleeping so well. She'd

tried and other than a few minutes off and on, she'd tossed around the small mattress a lot trying to keep her mind clear and not thinking about him. When they'd kissed, he'd picked her up like she weighed nothing. Being surrounded by muscle had done it for her and she would have consumed him if he hadn't stopped.

Gia wasn't a virgin; her cycle had taken care of that. Despite her father trying to keep her contained during that time, Walker had the compassion to help her sneak out and ease the insanity. She wasn't proud of it, going to an acquaintance for relief, but it was also part of their world.

Tilting her head, she let her gaze take a leisurely stroll over his body. She was practically salivating just looking at it. Mating or not, she still wanted him she decided. Very few males in her life caught her attention and none had as he did. Rising to her knees, she looked down at him. The thoughts in her head were ridiculous really, but she didn't care. He could reject her, again, but if she didn't try, she'd never know, right? It seemed like a logical theory, she decided.

Sucking in a quiet breath, her heart accelerated as she leaned down before she changed her mind. Placing a kiss on his mouth, she took his flavor into her again. His lips moved slightly as she did, so she repeated the action again. Deacon made a breathless moaning sound and shifted, his arm coming up behind her and surrounding her as their lips touched. Was he dreaming? She was breathless as excitement coursed through her. Leaning closer, she put her hand on his chest and was surprised at how warm his skin was, lowering her head, she pressed her lips against it. With slow movements, she kissed her way up his chest to his throat and then licked over it. Her animal was suddenly present inside her, coaxing her to continue. She felt emboldened by her own actions.

Shifting carefully in his arm, she moved up to sit on the edge of the cushion, there wasn't much room leftover with his large body covering it. Dropping the blanket, so she had both hands free, she touched his chest and bent down to kiss him again.

Deacon growled softly as their mouths touched and he shifted, dragging her across his body. His large hand grasped the back of her head as his mouth came to life under hers. He began kissing her roughly, setting her whole body ablaze as he did. Desperate to be closer to him, she twisted her hips and lay on what part of the cushion she could. With another animalistic sound, he turned, gripping her hip and dragging her tight against his body as he flipped to his side.

She ran her hands along his back, his shoulders, and any skin she could find as he commanded compliance with his mouth. This was insane, wanton and so hot that she felt like she was going to explode. Needing to feel skin on skin, she reached between them and yanked at her shirt, trying to move it. Deacon's hand shifted up under it and yanked it out of the way. She hissed out a breath against his mouth when her sensitive nipples rubbed against the hair on his chest.

Deacon growled low and forced a leg between hers, using it to shift her up higher, so his mouth could reach her throat. Gia's breath caught in her throat as his beard rubbed against her skin. Her body throbbed with need as she'd never felt before, not even when she was in the midst of her cursed cycle.

When he flipped onto his back and gripped her waist, holding her still, she opened her eyes and looked down to see him looking up at her. She could see the indecision on his face, the realization that he wasn't dreaming, and this was real. They stayed like that, only their breathing filling the quiet around them.

As he shifted, to sit, she thought, this is it, he's going to deny me again. He stood up, taking her with him, and moved over to the bed, holding her to him and not putting her down alone.

Deacon maneuvered his large body onto the bed, bringing her down with him. Neither of them spoke as he lay back, leaving her straddling his half-dressed body. Emboldened by her need, Gia grabbed her shirt and ripped it over her head, tossing it to the floor. This was her chance to show him how good they could be together, and she wasn't passing it up.

Before she could move, he gripped her waist and shifted her up, allowing his mouth to reach her breast. When his mouth closed over the taut nipple, she moaned deep in her throat. Sharp teeth scrapped over it as he sucked on it.

Grasping his hair, she jerked on his head and dragged his mouth to hers. He complied and attacked hers. Running her tongue along his sharp teeth, she felt a shudder go through her.

She found herself flipped onto her back and his weight pressed into her. Before she could wrap her legs around him, he moved down her body until he knelt on the floor. Grasping her by the back of her knees, he pulled her toward, him, holding her legs open. When his hot breath brushed over her sensitive sex, she gasped. Deacon's grip tightened as he licked over her once and then moaned loud.

Gia couldn't breathe as he kissed her between her legs. She'd never let a male do this to her before and the sensations going through her had her unable to breathe. She gripped the sheet in her hands and tried to get the leverage to rock into him, but his hands held her down on the bed, leaving her at his mercy.

"Deacon," she moaned, need burning through her. He growled low, his lips vibrating against her, then he bit her swollen flesh. The release crashed through her making her cry out. He didn't ease up, just held her down and kept doing it over and over again. Gia was losing her mind as wave after wave shook her body.

When he finally lifted his head, she couldn't move, her whole body was quivering as she tried to suck air into her lungs.

The bed shifted and she opened her eyes to see him kneeling over her. She moved her eyes slowly over his nakedness and whispered a moan. His body was male perfection. When she lifted her hand to touch him, he grasped it and dragged it over her head and then took her other hand and moved it so he could hold both in one hand. She squirmed from the look he was giving her. His steel-blue eyes were so dark, a look of possession in them that made her breath catch in her throat. Stretched out before him, his gaze moved down over her body as his chest rose and fell. If he didn't move soon, she was going to cry.

Lowering his body onto her, she sucked in a breath as their skin felt like flames had set them on fire. Deacon leaned down and kissed her, hard and rough. She could taste herself and was surprised that it turned her on even more.

When he lifted his head and looked down at her, she couldn't look away. He wedged his body between her legs and reached with his other hand, to move underneath her and lift her hips. He held her like that for what felt like hours. She was at his mercy, unable to move to push against him.

With a low growl, he thrust his hips and entered her in one hard move. She moaned when their bodies connected. Dropping his head, he looked down between their bodies as he pulled out and did it again. It was the most erotic moment of her life.

When his hand released hers, she moved fast to touch him before he could change his mind. She needed to touch him, all of him, to feel him beneath her hands. He hooked his elbow behind her knee and brought her leg up higher as his weight pinned her to the bed. A low growl was coming from him with each thrust, and it brought her to the brink of orgasm fast. His animal was close, this was them marking her as their own.

Gasping, she clung to him, unable to move with him but needing to feel closer to him. The taste of blood hit her tongue and she realized her mouth was full of sharp teeth. Her fox was that close, being called to the surface by his animal.

Deacon increased the pace and started pounding into her and Gia cried out as she went over the edge. Turning her head into his throat, she moaned, "mine," and then bit into his flesh.

An animal sound of triumph came from him as he stiffened over her, his hips jerking. Releasing his flesh, Gia tried to breathe. Her whole body was vibrating from the force of what had just happened.

Deacon turned his head and crushed her mouth with his.

She tasted him, blood, and herself, in her mind there would never be another moment in her life that was more perfect than now.

When he moved his head and rested it on the pillow, he slowly released her leg and let his weight settle over her. She didn't care if she couldn't move or breathe, she was content staying here like this forever.

After his breathing slowed, he shifted his hips and pulled out of her. Gia turned her head and saw the blood running down his skin, she licked over it slowly. She'd marked him as her mate and there wasn't the slightest feeling of regret.

Deacon lifted most of his weight off her, propping himself up on his elbows. His sexy eyes moved over her face with a softness she'd never seen in them before. With his fingertips, he brushed away the sweaty hair stuck to her face. "Did I hurt you?"

Licking her lips, she smiled, "no, I think you branded my soul though."

His lips quirked into a lopsided grin.

Gia watched the blood run down his neck.

"What did you do?" His tone was so soft it was barely spoken out loud.

"Marked you." She reached up and traced his mouth lightly.

"I know what, but why?" A pained look came over his face.

Gia didn't want sadness and reality right now, she wanted to savor this moment for as long as she could. "I don't want any skanky females to be thinking you're free for the taking." She gave him a playful grin.

He snorted softly and then dropped his forehead to rest on hers. "No chance of that." He kissed her and then pushed up, so their bodies were no longer touching.

The air sent a chill over her skin.

He held himself there and looked down at her. "I haven't even looked at another since I watched this fiery redhead hand fifteen guys their asses as she breezed across a finish line holding the pelt." He kissed her quickly on the mouth and then got up. "I'll heat the water for a shower."

She watched him walk over to the tank to turn it on, admiring the way the muscles flexed down his back and butt as he moved. His words sunk in. The fiery redhead was her and that was five years ago before she'd started defense training and taking control of her life. Sitting up, she pulled the sheet up around her. "Deacon, why did you never come to find me?"

He turned from the tank and looked at her. "I didn't want to ruin your life." He said it softly, truth-tinging every word.

"Wasn't that my call though?" She hugged her knees and watched him. She could tell him what her brother said, but didn't want to force it, she wanted him to come to her on his terms not because some bylaw said it was okay.

"Yeah, it was." He went over to the shelf and grabbed two bottles of water, then moved with silent grace over and held one out to her. She took it and he stood there looking down at her, "I checked in on you a lot, to see how you were doing." He opened the bottle and then looked at it, "I knew you were going to go places and I didn't want to get in your way."

She took a moment to have a few sips of the water, trying to figure out what that meant.

Before she could say anything else, he sighed, "look," he motioned to the bed, "I didn't," he grinned, it faded fast, "I'm not going to lie, I've thought about being with you for years, but despite you destroying my control, I don't want to spoil this with something that will end with you angry with me again." He looked at the door, "or me ending up like that bat."

Gia smirked, "he had it coming."

He nodded and looked back at her, "mmm, I have no doubt." He capped the bottle of water and then reached out his hand to her, "let's just enjoy right now as it is before reality sets in."

Setting down the bottle of water, she took his hand. "You know we're going talk about things."

"Oh, I know, sweetheart, and I also know it's not going to end the way either of us wants." He leaned down and kissed her mouth softly. "I'm still not going to ruin your life. Just, let's enjoy our moment in the dark before daylight interrupts us."

She didn't understand what he meant, but nodded and let him lead her toward the shower. None of that made sense. If he regretted it, why was he being so caring toward her? A moment in the dark? What happened when daylight came? Her legs felt like rubber, and she couldn't get her brain to kick back in. His scent was all over her, on her tongue, her lips, he was all she could smell. When he turned as they reached his little shower stall, all she could look at was her mark on his neck. Her fox was very happy with that mark. "Deacon."

He looked down at her as he reached into the shower.

"You don't regret it do you?" She felt juvenile and ridiculous looking at him with a pouty face, but she needed to know.

He looked at her for a moment, searching her face, then leaned down and kissed her. "No, I don't."

She could work with that; he wasn't being cold toward her. Despite wanting him to profess his devotion and mark her as his mate, she couldn't help feeling that he may have done right by her. Staying off her radar and out of her life all this time allowed her to become who she was now.

She let him lead under the water. If they mated anytime in the last five years, she wouldn't be on the team now or helping liberate her own kind.

With a gentle touch, he turned her, so her back was to him and began to gently wash her back.

Deacon Parrish had allowed her to choose her own path and she understood that now, but their paths were meant to be entwined and there was no turning that back now.

Calum's words came to her 'tell him to stop running.' She smiled and tilted her head back to rest against him.

His hands moved all over her, stirring her up again. As she turned around and stretched up to kiss him, she decided she'd let him run in circles around it for as long as it took—eventually he'd understand there was no way to outrun her and what they were to one another.

Chapter Twenty- Four

He stood there looking at the cabin, Giana was still sleeping. Rubbing his hands over his beard, Deacon dropped his head down to rest in them. *What did I do?* Last night, being with her was the most amazing and possibly stupidest thing he'd ever done in his life so far. Jerking his head up, he looked at the cabin again. He could see her beneath him, every time he closed his eyes now, pale, beautiful, and his. Only she wasn't officially 'his'.

Touching the mark on his neck for the hundredth time, he blew out a long breath. It hadn't healed when he'd shifted earlier. Part of him had wanted it to heal over, the other part was proud to wear her mark. Turning, he went back over to the truck, to repack his gear—that didn't need repacking.

She'd marked him. His heart had felt like it was going to explode in his chest when she'd done it. His animal had screamed in victory inside him. Currently, the creature was still mad that Deacon hadn't claimed her right then and there. He'd wanted to. He almost had. After he'd been afraid to move, afraid to be close to her for fear his animal would break through his control and do just that. Then he'd looked at her and his heart felt like it was stuck in his throat, she was so beautiful.

He slammed the door to the truck and then winced. Jerking around he looked at the cabin, hoping he hadn't woken her up. This was a clusterfuck beyond all others. The only thread of logic he was clinging to was the fact that 'mine' didn't really qualify as her accepting him and claiming him properly. He opened the door and then rested his forehead on the frame. "Keep telling yourself that and eventually, you might believe it." He couldn't walk away from her now. Which left him with another bigger problem, how could he be with her all the time without a repeat of last night and that would lead to marking her? Because he only had so much willpower and as he found out last night, Giana could smash through it without even trying.

Blowing out another breath, he opened the door again and reached behind the seat, he lifted the long case out. Cleaning his rifle was on today's list, along with just about anything else he could think of to keep busy and keep his hands off her. Setting the case on the hood, he went back and grabbed the smaller pack to get what he needed. Reaching in, he felt his phone, the one he wasn't supposed to use. *Fuck.*

Anytime he'd felt like he was losing his mind, he talked to Calum. The man always had some sort of answer that set his head straight.

Setting the bag beside his rifle case, he stomped over to where he'd put his run pack. Protocol be damned, if he didn't talk to someone about this, he was going to turn into a raging lunatic. Opening it as he went back to the truck, he pulled out the phone and brought up the emergency number. *This* qualified as an emergency.

He wasn't surprised to hear Illias on the other end.

"Deacon, it's Illias, what's happening?"

Closing his eyes, he tried not to sound like a lovesick idiot. "I need to contact Calum."

"Has something happened? I thought you'd be secure." Illias cursed a few times.

"We're secure."

"Thank fuck. You gave me a heart attack. Does it constitute an emergency? I've been told to not give out numbers unless it does."

Deacon raised an eyebrow, "you always follow the rules?"

Illias laughed, "no. Hang on."

Deacon breathed a sigh of relief that he didn't have to try to explain that he needed Calum to exercise the demons chasing his soul right now. He wrote down the number. "Any word on when we can go again?"

"I just have to wait for Fallen to find a safe, off-the-record location, so I'm hoping by tomorrow."

Deacon shoulders dropped with relief. One day, he could do that. He really needed his job to distract him right now. "Sounds good."

"Don't forget to check your six," Illias laughed, "I have no idea what that means, I heard it in a movie."

Deacon grinned, "I'm watching my back, don't worry."

"Ah, got it." The line went dead.

"One more day." He mumbled as he punched in Calum's number.

"Hello?"

"It's me." Now that he had him on the other end, he had no idea what to say to him.

"Deacon, is everything all right? I'm assuming you got this number from Illias?"

"Yeah, I did." He closed his eyes, "everything is not all right, it's a fucking mess."

"Oh?"

"She marked me, Cal, last night. I was a weak idiot and gave into her and—" he stopped; he couldn't think about that right now.

"I see."

"A mate's mark." He clarified.

"I figured that." Calum cleared his throat. "I take it you didn't claim her."

"Yeah, I mean no, I didn't. You know why I can't."

"Listen, I know you've spent years telling yourself that, but there are other things you need to be aware of..."

"I know, I know, it works itself out and all that, but Cal, none of that changes the fact that she's from an Alpha bloodline and I'm a," he waved his hand around, "mutt."

Calum chuckled quietly, "are you going to let me talk?"

Deacon scowled at the ground, "sure." There was nothing he could say that would clear it all up. *Nothing.*

"Okay, I told you I looked into your family and history..."

The cabin door opened, and a sleepy, sexy-looking Gia stepped out and smiled at him. "I have to go. Giana's awake." He hung up the phone and jammed it back in his pack.

"Any news?" She stretched and then brushed her hair back from her face.

Deacon swallowed, trying to get his words to work. She looked so beautiful; the early dawn light seemed like it was only highlighting her. "Uh, probably have a plan by tomorrow." He jolted into action and spun back to his rifle, "Illias is just trying to find us an off-the-grid safe house to work out of."

"That's good news," her voice told him she was moving toward him, "that we'll be getting more people out."

He glanced to see she was right behind him now. He motioned to his rifle, "I need to clean this and check the sight, make sure it's ready."

She touched his arm and ran her hand softly over it, "do you want me to get breakfast started?"

He looked down at her, her sleepy eyes were looking at him with such a tender look, his heart beat out of rhythm for a few pumps. He smiled, "that would be great."

"Okay." She stretched up and kissed his lips softly, then turned and went back toward the cabin.

He stood there like a statue and watched her go back in. Reflex had him lick over his lips, taking the taste of her into his mouth. *Fuck.* He was in so much trouble here. Life-altering, can't-walk-it-back kind of trouble.

~

Deacon watched her head into the bush to go for a run. He was both disappointed and relieved she chose to wait until she was out of sight to strip down. He felt like a complete dick, turning her down again for a run together. It was bad enough he'd babbled all through breakfast about the importance of keeping her weapon clean. She'd sat there and listened, asking questions, the whole time those sexy fucking eyes were eating him up like a tasty snack. His own traitorous body seemed to be wired to respond to her now, one look and he was hard, his brain turned off, his animal anticipating. He'd practically run from the cabin like a coward, saying he needed to get the porch floor fixed or mice would get in.

He needed to get his head together before they were back with the team, lives depended on him focusing, not to mention that he dreaded having his ass handed to him by Wynter if he screwed up.

A squirrel ran across the path and then froze and looked at him. "What? You never have a bad day?" Its tail twitched a few times and then it took off. *Great. Just fucking wonderful*, he was talking to squirrels now.

More than once since he'd woke to her warm body against his, he'd asked himself why he hadn't taken the out Wynter offered. It would have been the easiest solution, orders to go elsewhere. Bam. Done, no arguments and hurt feelings, but—

Scowling, he stomped toward the shed, his every thought came with a *but* now.

If he'd taken Wynter's offer, he never would have felt her skin against him, heard the sounds she made when he was inside her—*fuck*.

He just, the idea of other members of this team watching over her wasn't right. It was for him to do.

His animal stirred, he was not feeling kindly about not being around her—he was good with Konner and most of the rest of his team, but would lose his mind if she was partnered with another male.

It had been torture to lay in bed with her while she was sleeping, but he couldn't bring himself to get up and leave her.

His animal was at the point of pushing the claiming before he got out of the bed and stumbled outside.

Rubbing the back of his neck to try and release some tension, he dragged his hand over the mark on his flesh. She'd marked him for all to know. A lump formed in his throat and his chest tightened at the same time. He looked in the direction she'd gone. *Fuck.* Putting his rifle back in the case and his gear away, he put it all back into the truck and locked the door.

Grabbing his run pack, he slung it over his head and turned away from the direction she'd gone, he would circle around and go check the traps. The exercise would do him some good, keep his body busy until his mind wore itself out replaying the events that happened in the dark.

Chapter Twenty-Five

Gia glanced at the phone sitting beside Deacon's plate, he'd looked at it more than twenty times in the last half hour. When they'd sat down a message had come through, it was one number, nothing more. Illias had sent the key that Deacon would need to figure out the message they were going to send. Neither of them had expected the second message to take this long.

He hadn't said more than five words during that time either. He had been trying all day to stay clear of her, and she had given him his space, not pushing for more. She'd known the risks the night before. It was hard not to push him though, the entire day he'd kept moving from one thing to the next without pause. Checking the traps, cleaning the kills, stretching the pelts, preparing the cabin for winter, and a dozen other things. The only thing that helped her to silently endure it was the look he kept giving her when he didn't think she was watching. His actions were saying one thing, but his heart was telling him something different. Gia was content with that, eventually, emotions had a way of overcoming internal objections.

Pushing her plate away, she smirked at him. "If they wanted our undivided attention, they succeeded."

He picked up the phone and looked at it once more. "It's a

lot of moving pieces to keep track of.”

"Do you think we're going back to the same area?"

Placing his fork on the plate, he stood up and picked up their dishes. "I don't know. Tomas has to know we found one of their houses by now," he went over to the counter and set them in the basin, "not to mention one of their lackey's entire group is missing."

She watched him hesitate, trying to decide if he was sitting down again or washing the dishes. Getting up, she went over and picked up the kettle to check how much water was in it and put it back on the stove. "I don't know about you, but I'm going to need some coffee to get through waiting."

He smirked, "hopefully the next message comes tonight."

Gia spun around, "they wouldn't keep us in suspense *that* long, would they?"

He shrugged, "it's been known to happen."

With her hands on her hips, she looked around the cabin, "well I'm out of things to do to kill that much time..."

The phone beeped and they both turned to stare at it.

"Showtime." He whispered and went back over and picked it up. "A phone number." He sat down and opened the small notebook.

Gia stood behind him and looked over his shoulder as he figured out the right order of it. He did it so fast that she wasn't able to figure out how it worked.

When he dropped the pen, he glanced up at her for a moment, there was something in that look that made her heart ache. She felt it too. Calling the number meant their time here alone was over. "Call it," she said softly.

He dialed the number and then hit the speaker button.

"Ding, ding, ding. You are the winner and the first call on our new hotline." Illias sang into the other end. "I'm going to put you on hold, Deacon," he cleared his throat, "and partner, until the others call in and then we'll all be linked into one big happy group call."

"We'll be here." Deacon told him, then got up and got the coffee down off the shelf.

Gia stood where she was, looking at the phone. "I don't understand any of the technical stuff," she admitted.

Deacon paused as he measured out the coffee, "I don't even try to", he shrugged, "the tech team," he glanced at her, "or whatever they're called is one more specialist team of the Alliance."

"I didn't know there was a whole team."

Moving over to the stove, he set the percolator on it and picked up the kettle. "I think Calum told me there are fifteen specialist teams that work through the Alliance."

Gia looked back down at the phone, "I guess I never thought of the logistics of everything."

"It's not for us to think about, we have our jobs and are just one piece of a very big machine." He turned around and started to pour the water into the filter at the top of the percolator.

Gia took a deep breath and let it out slowly, trying to steady her nerves. Standing idle and waiting for anything was not one of her strengths.

"Hail, hail the gangs all here." Illias sounded so amused.

"Do we have everyone?" That was Devin.

"All present and accounted for, even our new addition, Konner Flores."

"All right, everyone, we have a lot to cover and are trying to keep the call as short as possible," Devin said.

"Take all the time you need, not even god can hear what we're saying," Illias added quickly.

"This is the number you will use for contact. From here Illias can put you through to anyone else on this team—we'll be using that for now until we test his team's other idea." Devin paused.

Gia glanced to see Deacon was still making the coffee, but his posture told her he was paying attention to every word.

"Beginning tomorrow, all of you will be heading back down to the border."

"Location?" York asked.

"You'll get the final location once you're closer." Calum's level tone informed everyone. "We've had to rearrange the order of plans due to some movement."

"They moved some of the captives to another state," Jesse added.

That got Deacon's attention, he turned from the stove and came over to the table crossed his arms, and stared at the phone.

"We've had to put more teams into play," Calum continued, "but rest assured all we were watching are still under surveillance." He said the last part with emphasis, making Gia wonder which of the group it was directed to.

"We've had to employ new protocol for almost every aspect of the Alliance, so on your trip back, all of you will have stops along the way to get in touch with the clans along your route." Calum paused.

Gia exchanged a look with Deacon, it was just sinking in that whatever had compromised their team was affecting all clans under the Alliance's protection.

"The clans will have to abandon all electronic forms of communication for now," Illias was now speaking, "a new number has been set up, the same way as this one for them to use to get in touch with anyone connected to the Alliance, including the King himself."

Deacon rubbed his hand over his beard and then turned to grab the cups. His movement was tense, no doubt from what he was hearing.

"All of you are going to have to adjust your routes to stop and get this number to the clans, they've been sitting there in the dark since our last communication." Devin's tone was low and uneven.

"With that in mind," Jesse was now speaking, making Gia wonder if some of them were all together somewhere, "we're going to have to keep unnecessary communication to a minimum until the tech team finds a secure way to handle a larger volume of calls."

"We're working with god-like speed." Illias told him, "Even *the* all-mighty took seven days, we've only had a few so far."

Deacon came over and held out a cup to her, he was

smirking.

"Pen and paper ready, boys and girls? I'm going to be listing this off fast," Illias warned them. Gia set the cup down and sat down. Taking his notebook, she sat ready to write anything necessary.

"Adjust your routes however you like to reach all of these along the way." Jesse said, "we have the rest of the co-ord team and some others out there right now filling in the gaps."

Gia kept her head down, her eyes on the notebook in front of her.

"First up, Deacon and Gia, you need to pick up Konner at..."

Gia wrote the numbers down quickly and then looked up at Deacon. He nodded, so he knew what they meant.

"The clans you're popping in to see are Roberson Clan, Harmon Clan, and Marin Clan. The number they are to use will be sent to you, in the same manner this one was."

Gia dropped the pen and looked at what she'd written. They were going to have to go see her father. She couldn't focus on what Illias was saying now, she'd stopped listening as soon as he said York's name.

Getting up, she looked up at Deacon and then back down to the notebook. He had the same shell-shocked look on his face as she felt.

By the time the call ended, Gia had done at least twenty laps around the inside of the room.

She watched Deacon hang up the phone and then tuck it into his pocket.

"So, they're sending the map coordinates for our destination?" She hadn't been able to focus on the rest of the instructions.

He nodded. "Rather than say locations over the phone." He crossed his arms over his chest and braced his legs wider. "Illias' team is good, but if they're this cautious, something *really* serious has happened."

Gia looked at the notepad. "I know two of those clans, obviously." She rolled her eyes, still trying to accept that they were sending her to her own clan. "I guess they aren't aware how rocky things are with my family." She said more to herself than to him.

"The list would have been made going off everyone's location."

Sighing, she looked at the ceiling. She hadn't considered that. "I am not looking forward to it." She looked back over at him, he hadn't moved a muscle.

He started to say something when his phone rang. Pulling it out, he tapped the screen and then leaned down and started writing numbers down.

When he finished, she moved over and looked at it. "Why so many numbers?"

He tapped the first line, "clan locations, and I'm going to say the last one is where we're swapping vehicles."

"That makes sense. I don't think I need a map to find my father though."

Deacon gave her a gentle look, "I'll go get my map."

She spun around and looked at him, "Deacon?"

He paused, holding the door open.

"Should we head out tonight or first thing tomorrow?"

Letting the door close, he looked at her for a moment and then around the cabin. Gia noticed his gaze hesitated when he looked at his bed. "That's your call." He pointed to the water tank. "I just have to drain the lines and lock up the windows before we go."

Gia nodded, then slowly turned and looked right at the bed. He wouldn't be joining her in it tonight, she already knew that as a fact. "We can take turns driving and rest in the van."

"All right. Just let me get the map and we'll sketch out a route." His tone was quiet, almost contemplative.

When he was gone, she looked around more slowly. She wanted to come here when the team took a break. Zeroing in on the dishes, she sighed and went over to turn the water heater on to wash them. "Run until you can't run anymore," she whispered as she stacked the dishes in the small basin, "I'll be right here when you stop."

Chapter Twenty-Six

Deacon glanced at her as they turned the last corner to her clan's village, she had a white-knuckle grip on her hat. Giana hadn't said much since they'd left his cabin. They took turns driving, listened to the radio, and only stopped for a quick bite or gas. He should be happy she wasn't trying to discuss what had happened between them, but now he just wanted her to *talk*. His animal was almost as tense as she was, fretting because their mate was unhappy.

Giving her another quick look, he slowed and pulled the van off the road. Giana looked over at him, a questioning look on her face. Putting it in park, he turned and looked at her. "What's wrong?"

She closed her eyes for a moment and sighed. When she opened them, he was surprised to see anger in them. "The last time I saw my parents it didn't end well."

He raised an eyebrow, "because you were leaving?"

"That and why I was leaving." She slumped back in the seat and stared out the window.

"They don't want you on the team?"

She snorted, "they don't want me doing anything but being a perfect, pretty Alpha's daughter."

"Your job with Jesse is important," he motioned between them, "what the teams are doing together now is even more so, we're rescuing our kind."

"I know. They get that too—they just don't want *me* to be part of it."

"I thought it was just Nox, being himself." He said quietly.

"No. Nox's opinion of what I do is the popular consensus of my entire family."

"I thought one of your brothers was on your side."

"Walker?" She looked down at her hat, "he is, but he works with our clan, so he can't make his thoughts known or his life would be hell." She shrugged, "I get that." Tossing the hat on the dash, she turned and looked at him, "my father called the king to have me removed from the team."

Deacon didn't know what to say to that.

"He ended up getting Devin who sided with me." She motioned to the road in front of them, "my brother was removed from the special operations because of me," she shook her head, "I'm going to be walking into a battle, trust me."

"If the prince wants you on the team, your father can't have you removed." He didn't understand what it was to have parents that fought for you, or in her case, against what she wanted. "I didn't know it was that bad." He said quietly.'

Gia turned to look at him, "most think life is perfect when you are part of an Alpha family," she shrugged, "maybe it is for some, but not me."

"I can go in and give him the number."

She laughed, "oh that will go over even better." Her gaze moved to his neck, "when my father senses my scent blended with yours, and yet I'm hiding in the van."

His hand went to the bite scar on his neck. "It's a little late for him to object."

"And you're ready for the conversation about why I don't have a mark?" She closed her eyes and sighed, "look, I get that you have—reservations about it, I do, even if they're not really warranted, I'm still respecting your feelings on it." She sighed and then pointed out the window, "he will not, and it won't just be him," she shook her head, it's never just him, "two of my brothers are Alpha's in training," she made exaggerated quote symbols in the air, "so they're going to be all up in our faces too."

"What's between us, is no one else's business, Giana."

The stressed look on her face, eased slightly, "you are the only person that doesn't make me cringe when you use my full name, did you know that?"

He shook his head. "No, but the fact remains that this is between us and no one else."

"I wish that were true." She blew out a breath, "this is going to be awful."

"I don't care what your father has to say, we're doing our job and then we have to move on to the next and pick up Konner." Those eyes that felt like they were branding his soul every time she looked at him, moved over his face with a soft caressing look.

"I don't want you in the middle of it, Deacon, my family problems."

He tried to shrug it off playfully, "as you know I have my own problems," he smirked, "you have no issue with all of my," he waved his hand around, "*issues*, so a few barked words won't bother me." The anxiety coming from her was almost crippling him, his animal was angry, and wanted blood. Reaching over, he took her hand and held it in his until she looked back to his eyes. "I will do anything to protect you, from anyone." He hadn't intended the growl in his voice, but his animal wanted his say in this too.

Squeezing his hand, she nodded, a jerky motion at first but then he saw the resolve come back in her expression. "Let's get it over with."

Lifting her hand, he kissed it before releasing it and turning in his seat. "Just have a little faith, sweetheart, growling Alpha types I'm used to," he glanced at her quickly before pulling back onto the road, "I work with your brother, remember?"

Gia grinned, "well, you're about to meet version one and

three of him, they're more polite than Nox is, but worse in other ways."

The village was larger than he had thought it would be. In all the years of keeping informed about her, he never thought to look into her clan. If he were anyone else, he might feel intimidated, but after what he'd been through to prove himself and get on the team, there was nothing they could do or say that would phase him. His creature was close to the surface but working with his feelings and not fighting with him about their mate for once. He knew that they'd have to go into this with a united front to get Giana through it and back on the road.

She pointed to a street, "main house is at the end of this."

"You're sure he'll be there?"

She nodded, "the offices are beside it, but he works from the house most of the time unless it's an official thing."

Her voice was strained, but she had steeled her spine and was ready to face them. He was proud of her at that moment. He always was, now that he thought of it, but now more than ever. He had no idea what she'd been through to get to this point and doubted many others would have pushed through the struggle to last. Amari, the other Alpha female on her team, was an entirely different type of 'Alpha's daughter.' Giana was softer, more compassionate and he meant what he'd said, he would protect her no matter what. Even if the threat was her own family.

When he turned off the van, he looked over to see her tucking her hair up under her hat. Reaching for his own, he turned it around backward, he wanted no obstruction for others to see the expression in his eyes if they crossed a line. "Ready?"

She nodded and opened the door.

Deacon got out and his hand automatically went to the sidearm on his leg. He wouldn't shoot anyone but keeping his hand close to it tended to make people think before doing something stupid.

Giana came around the front of the van and raised an

eyebrow as she looked at his hand, "you can't shoot them." She said quietly.

He shrugged, "should I bring the tranq gun?" She smiled and that was much better to see than the hesitant expression. He motioned for her to lead the way.

As they walked up the long walkway, a man came out of the buildings beside the house. Deacon didn't have to guess if he was part of her family, his red hair was the exact color of hers.

He walked with long strides toward her, a big smile on his face. "Well, this day just got better."

Giana turned and darted over to him, throwing her arms around him.

Deacon paused; a feeling of jealousy filled him. He had to reassure his animal that this was her brother, and judging by her reaction it was Walker, her only ally in her tense world.

Releasing her, Walker gave Deacon a quick once over and then looked down at her, "why are you here?"

"Official business," she told him, then motioned to Deacon, "we're bringing new contact information to the clans on our way back to work."

Walker nodded his head slowly, "does that information come with explanations? Because I have to tell you writing in notebooks instead of on my computer is getting old fast."

Deacon stepped over, closer to Gia, to placate his creature, "we can offer few answers at this point."

Walker held his look for a moment and then nodded and motioned to the house, "let the games begin."

Giana started walking again, "how is he?"

"Pissed, not just because of you, but all this hush-hush shit is getting on everyone's nerves." He stopped her in front of the door. "Nox told them someone followed you and tried to take you."

Giana's shoulders slumped. "Nox should learn to keep his mouth shut." She looked down the step to Deacon, then back to her brother. "Is he here?"

Walker shook his head, "no he was called back yesterday and took off out of here."

Gia looked relieved.

Deacon stepped into the house behind them and closed the door. He paused to look around. It wasn't elaborately decorated like he'd imagined it would be. The face that Giana had been content at his cabin surprised him though.

"You want me to go get him?" Walker asked her in a hushed tone.

Giana nodded but said nothing for a moment. "I don't live here anymore, remember?"

Deacon frowned, the riff with her family had been serious enough that she'd left home? Where was she living then? His animal prompted her to move closer to her.

As Walker disappeared around the corner, a woman started to come down the stairs. She was an older version of Giana.

"Giana?" The woman smiled at her, the look fading when she noticed Deacon. "Is everything all right?"

Gia took a step and then stopped. "Everything is fine. This," she motioned to him, "is my partner, Deacon, he's on the same team as Nox."

Her mother smiled again, a polite, forced one. "You're here on business?"

Deacon nodded, "yes 'mam, the Alliance has us visiting all of the clans delivering information from the king."

A look of surprise replaced the fake smile. "Do you travel with my daughter?"

Giana nodded, "They have us paired with members of the incursion team now," She glanced at Deacon, an impatient look in her eyes, "after they tried to take Jesse's mate."

Deacon realized she was trying to keep the attention from her.

"Are you able to stay for tea?"

Deacon watched Giana stiffen. "I'm afraid not, Mom, we have other clans to go see today."

"Of course." She moved down the stairs. "I'll go see if Oren is free."

"Walker went to get him," Gia said quietly.

Her mother paused. "We'll wait in the office then, rather

than stand in the entranceway."

Giana gave him a quick glance and followed her mother down the hall.

Whatever he'd thought her life was like, he was realizing how wrong he'd been, this felt like a war zone, not a home.

Giana's mother led them into a large office. It was decorated with dark wood and much fancier furnishings than what he'd seen of the house.

She turned and looked up at him. "I'm sorry, I didn't even introduce myself." She held out her hand, "Dani Marin."

Deacon moved closer and grasped her hand lightly. He bowed his head in a brief polite acknowledgment of her status before letting her hand go. "Deacon Parrish, 'mam." When he lifted his chin again, he noticed she was looking at his neck.

She inhaled a deep breath and then gave him a polite smile. "I'll go see what's keeping your father." With barely a look at Giana, she walked out and closed the door.

Giana sent him a quick look of panic. "She knows." She whispered.

"She didn't say anything, so don't panic—before we need to." He added quickly. The anxiety was coming off of her in waves. He went over to her and put his hand on the side of her neck. Using his thumb to tip up her chin, so she was looking at him again, he held her eyes with his own. "Where's that girl that breezes over the finish line because she's confident in her abilities?"

"She's standing in her father's office." Her voice was quiet.

He nodded, "on official business, not at his daughter." Deacon watched until she gave him a slight nod. "Okay." Touching her cheek softly, he dropped his hand away. The last thing they needed was him kissing her when her father walked in and right now that's what he wanted to do, kiss her until she was distracted from the fear and anxiety that was rolling off her.

"He'll be waiting for Nash and Vance." She said and then took a deep breath, exhaling loudly. "It's always the three of them when I'm involved."

Deacon didn't say a word for a moment, he needed to override the anger that hit him like a punch in the gut. It pissed him off that they would do that. He could just picture three men towering over her. "You have me this time." He smiled at her, hoping the anger was buried deep enough it wasn't visible.

Before she could speak, the door opened, and an older version of Nox walked in. The way he walked into the room left no question that he was in charge. Deacon often wondered why Nox had this arrogant air about him, now he knew why. Behind Giana's father, two men came in, both resembled their sire with dark auburn hair. Dani followed and went to sit in a chair near the corner of the room.

Walker was the last to come into the room. He closed the door and then leaned against it. He watched his sister, not the men positioning themselves opposite her.

Deacon noted he had at least five inches on the tallest of them, not that he was measuring, but it was a false comfort to know he had some kind of advantage. They weren't tiny men, by any means, all were solidly built.

Her father gave Giana a hard look.

Taking her hat off, she cleared her throat, then looked at Deacon, "this is my partner, Deacon, he's part of the incursion team." She kept her gaze on his, "Deacon, this is my father, Oren," she motioned to the first one that walked in, "and my brothers Nash and Vance." She turned back to her father, "we're here on behalf of the Alliance."

Deacon stepped over to the desk and inclined his head the way Calum had almost had to beat into him. "Sir." Reaching into his pocket, he pulled out a slip of paper and held it out. "Due to a breach of the Alliance's system, you're to use this number. They will explain the new protocols to you when you call."

Her father took the piece of paper opened it and looked at the number. "What of our phones, are they secure?"

"I don't know the details regarding private phones, sir," Deacon motioned to the paper, "they'll have all the answers for you."

Her father nodded his head slowly and then looked across the desk at Giana. "You're driving to every clan to bring them this information?"

Giana nodded, "there are many teams out doing it."

Oren Marin looked from her slowly to Deacon, he noted the gun his hand rested on. With a hard look on his face, he turned back to Giana. "Nox told us you'd almost been taken."

Giana gave Deacon a quick look, "Nox shouldn't be discussing things with people unless he's been authorized to do so." Her tone was a lot more respectful than Deacon would have managed.

"I'm your father and an Alpha with the Alliance."

"I know, Dad, but someone has been sharing information and helping Aiden Tomas' organization from *within* the Alliance members—so discussing anything without clearance is a problem."

She wasn't wrong. Deacon felt a tinge of pride by the way she was holding her own.

"Is this true?" Dani asked quietly.

Oren nodded. "Shepard gave me a heads up a few weeks ago, that something was happening."

Her mother looked quickly back to Gia, "should you be involved in this."

Giana took a deep breath and blew it out. Deacon noticed she looked to Walker before she held her chin up and answered her mother. "It's no different than what's been happening since before I was born, Mom."

"They almost took you," Nash said.

Giana shook her head, "no they didn't. They never would have found me. Jesse said if Deacon hadn't been there, he probably wouldn't have."

Everyone in the room turned to look at him.

"You were under the ground, weren't you?" Walker asked.

Giana shrugged, then turned back to her mother, "I was alone that time," she pointed to Deacon, "now I'm not. The Co-ord team travels with a member of the incursion team everywhere they go now."

"I don't think it's a good idea for you to continue with this," Nash waved his hand around, "ridiculous fantasy of working for the coordination team."

His animal was poised for a fight, and he didn't blame him. Deacon wasn't doing much better.

"It's a good thing I don't need your permission then, isn't it?" She put her hands on her hips and looked around the room. "In case you forgot, I'm an adult and able to make my own decisions."

Tension filled the room so suddenly that Deacon had to force his hand to move away from his gun and focus on keeping his animal under control.

"That's enough." Her father said, using that tone only an Alpha could get away with. He turned to Nash and held out the paper with the number on it. "You and Vance go over to the offices, use the landline and call this. Find out the protocol going forward. If our cell phones aren't to be used, find out what is acceptable."

Nash took it and nodded. He gave Giana a hard look and turned on his heel.

Walker opened the door and stood holding it as they went out of it.

"If you'll excuse us, my mate and I would like a word with our daughter."

Deacon looked at Giana, he searched her eyes for a moment, there was no fear or self-doubt in them.

She nodded her head slightly. "I won't be long."

Deacon inclined his head to her father and went over to the door. When he stepped out, Walker followed and closed the door behind them.

"Never a dull moment when my sister is home."

Deacon glanced at him to acknowledge he'd heard, then looked back at the door.

"So, funny thing, I didn't sense that Gia was mated, but," he made a point of looking at Deacon's neck, "it looks like you've been claimed."

Rubbing his hand over his beard, Deacon tried to figure out

how to answer. Walker stood there, watching him with interest. There wasn't a trace of the judgemental look the other two brothers had given him. He was different. He was important to Giana.

"I'm actually relieved to see you're thinking this through instead of spouting off something that will piss me off and force me to deck you," he looked at Deacon's weapon, "and probably get shot as a result." He gave him a lopsided grin.

"I can see why Giana speaks highly of you." Deacon told him in a distracted way. He was still trying to contain his animal side and hear if Giana needed him on the other side of the thick door. Before he could offer him some sort of answer to his question, his phone buzzed in his pocket. "Excuse me." Pulling it out, he hit the button to answer it, thankful for the interruption. "Yeah?" He cringed, probably not the best way to answer, considering the Prince of the Alliance could be on the other end.

"That sounds like a mood." It was Calum.

"Yeah, it's turning out to be that kind of day."

"Where are you?"

"Giana's clan." Deacon glanced at the door again.

"Ah, I understand the tone now. Her father is of the old school variety."

"I noticed." He watched the door, wishing she would come out of the room so the urge to kick it down would subside.

"I'll keep it short then, I wanted to finish the last conversation you hung up on."

He scowled, trying to think through the moment's tension to remember what the conversation was. It came back to him; he'd been freaking out about Giana marking him. "Oh, that." He said, moving a few more feet from Walker.

"There are some things you don't know that I should have told you a long time ago, but you had enough shit to wade through at that time."

"What are you talking about?" Deacon rubbed the back of his neck, trying to release some of the tension.

There was a long pause, "Shit. I'll call you right back, we

have to do this the proper way." He hung up.

Deacon looked at the phone. Do what right? Had something happened that would affect the operation? Tucking the phone back in his pocket, he turned back to face the door and Walker.

Walker gave him a curious look.

Deacon shook his head, "I don't even know."

The door opened and Giana came out. The expression on her face told him how well that conversation went. Not well at all.

A door opposite the office door opened and a teen boy came running in. "Walker." He gasped for a breath, "Zariah and her sister are trapped down by the gorge," he took a ragged breath, "by a bear, I don't know what's wrong with it."

Walker jolted and ran into the office.

Giana looked at the boy and ran down the hall to the front of the house. She went out the door.

Deacon caught up to her and put his arm out to stop her. "Where's the gorge?"

She pointed.

Turning he looked to where she pointed, "how far?"

"If you go down to the end of that street, there's a drop-off that leads down to it." Giana watched Walker come running out, he took off in a different direction than she'd pointed. "Walker's going down the trail." She grabbed his arm, "a fox isn't a match for a bear." Her voice shook.

Deacon nodded and jogged to the van, he opened it reached in, and grabbed her run pack. "Go," he tossed it to her, "wait," pulling his shirt over his head, he gave her a quick look, "use this when you shift back."

She caught the shirt. "What are you going to do?"

Deacon opened the side door and pulled out his rifle. "I'll deal with the bear."

Giana nodded, then turned and took off running.

Slipping the case over his shoulder, Deacon ran full out down the street she'd pointed to.

Chapter Twenty-Seven

When he reached the end of the street, he stepped over the rail and looked over the edge, he couldn't see anyone from here. Dropping to his knee, he opened the case and took out his rifle and ammo. Standing he looked around, a tall tree caught his eye. No time to debate it, he thought. Going back over to the other side of the railing, he went over and looked up it. Swinging the rifle to hang flat down his back, he started climbing the old pine? He had no idea what type of tree it was, just that it had a lot of branches that would enable him to go up it fast. The branches were close enough at the bottom that it was almost like going up a ladder. He moved swiftly, ignoring the scrapes along his bare skin. Giving up his shirt may not have been the smartest plan, but Giana parading around naked in front of others was more important and by now half the village would know what was happening.

Pausing, he looked in the direction Giana had pointed out to him, he could see movement down there now. Going up a few more feet he turned and wedged his body between the branches. This was going to be a whole new challenge, to balance his weight and the rifle and not fall out.

With cautious movements, he brought the rifle around and

awkwardly loaded it. Raising it up, he was able to use another branch as a support as he leaned his head down to see through the scope. He saw a flash of rust red and then moved it ahead of where the fox was running. He tensed when he got the wild animal in his sight, they needed to slow down, or they were going to reach it before he took it out. It was huge, and the boy had been right, it was angry and lashing out. The way it was weaving around, was going to make getting a good shot hard.

Deacon blew out a breath, centering himself as he made careful adjustments trying to predict the animal's movement. The bear stopped and reared on its hind legs; Deacon squeezed the trigger. He didn't pause to see if he'd downed, it, just loaded another round in with a well-practiced move. When it was loaded again, he brought the bear back into his sights. It was down, but still alive. Adjusting his aim for the animal's head, he squeezed the trigger. The sound of the shot was still echoing when the animal stopped moving.

Blowing out a breath, he moved the rifle slowly, looking for the children, he spotted them on top of a boulder, huddled together. The one was probably around twelve and the girl she was hugging looked to be six or seven. He closed his eyes for a second, waiting for the heavy feeling in the pit of his stomach to settle, and then moved it back to the bear. Walker was there, on the other side of it looking it over. Giana darted past him, wearing only his shirt, and ran to the kids.

His phone vibrating had him almost slip off the branch he was standing on. *Great timing, Calum,* he thought, shifting so he could reach to get it out of his pocket. He braced his shoulder on the branch and hit the button to answer it.

"Not a good time, Cal, I'm twenty feet up a tree, being stupidly heroic to save some kids from a bear."

"Did you?"

Deacon jolted it was not Calum on the other end.

"Save the children?"

"Yeah," he said slowly.

"Then I'd say it was more heroic than stupid." There was a pause, "it's Shepard Addison, I was told it was time for us to have a talk. Is this a bad time?"

Deacon looked toward the gorge, then to the ground, "sorry sir, I thought it was Calum calling me back."

"I gathered that. Calum called me. We've been keeping something from you for a long time and the time has come to tell you."

Deacon adjusted his footing.

"Would you like to get out of the tree first before I continue?"

"Ah," Deacon braced his shoulder against the limb and moved his rifle off the branch, "it might be a good idea, sir."

"Very well. I'll call you back in two minutes." The line went quiet.

Swearing softly, Deacon jammed the phone into his back pocket and moved the rifle to hang down his back again. What the hell was he talking about? He went down the tree so fast, barely taking the time for his footing to be sure enough before he moved to the next. He felt the bark and hardened sap dragging along his flesh but didn't have the time to slow down.

His boots hit the ground together as he jumped to the ground. Pulling the rifle off his shoulder, he went over the railing to put it in the case. Turning he saw a small group had gathered and was watching him, he hadn't even noticed them on the way down.

When the phone buzzed again, he turned his back to them and looked out over the landscape as he answered it.

"Hello."

"Both feet on the ground now?"

"Yes, sir." Deacon glanced down the front of him to see spots of blood from the branches on his chest.

"Good. Before I offer explanations, I'd like to make it clear that Calum was already championing for you to be under the Alliance's protection before we knew all the details. I'm sure you know he placed you under his protection the moment he found you."

"Yes, sir, I knew that." Why Calum had done that, he still didn't know. At the start Deacon had been nothing but a rude, mouthy, ungrateful brat, but Calum still gave him a chance.

"We still weren't certain until Calum did further research into your past and of course after he witnessed you shifting in person."

Deacon scowled at the ground. "I'm not following, sir."

"We didn't tell you sooner because Calum didn't want it to influence you and change who you were becoming."

Deacon had no idea what he was talking about, none whatsoever.

"The clan breed your mother was from, what you are, son, is very rare now. We have only ever had one other on record in North America."

"What does that have to do with me, sir?" Deacon tapped his hat against his leg to remove the dried pine needles from it.

"Calum shared with me the reservations you've been having—regarding your mate."

Deacon's breath left his body all at once. He'd called Giana's father, his chest tightened, was he about to be forbidden from being near Giana?

"You're concerned because you have the traits and appearance of your mother's clan and not your fathers, is that correct?"

"Something like that." He was struggling with why Calum would *ever* share any of this with the King of the Alliance. *Why?*

"I can hear the confusion in your voice, so let me summarize this for you. If once mated to Miss Marin, any more of your kind that turns up, they will be part of your clan. You will have a clan of your own to lead, Mister Parrish."

Deacon closed his eyes for a second and then opened them. "I don't want a clan—"

"That's a common feeling with new Alpha's son, believe me, many don't want to be in charge of a clan either." There was a slight pause, the silence was tense. "I'll leave you something to think about," another pause, Deacon wanted him to just spit it all out. "Without you establishing a maned wolf clan here in North America, any others found will be clan less and classified as rogue wanderers…"

Deacon swore every cuss word he could think of in his mind. "I get the picture, sir."

"I thought you would." The king sounded amused. "Giana Marin's Alpha bloodline is no longer an obstacle if you accept this, you'll be the first Alpha of your kind under the protection of the Alliance."

Deacon opened his mouth but couldn't find the words to say. Turning, he saw Giana and Walker coming toward him. She still wore his shirt but had stopped along the way to put her leggings back on. She sent him an inquisitive look. He shrugged because he honestly didn't know what was happening.

"I've rendered you speechless."

Deacon dragged his gaze from her. "I don't know what to say, sir."

The king chuckled. "Humble, I like that. I'm starting to see what Calum has been talking about. I just ask that you consider it, son—and thank you for climbing that tree and saving the children, and for everything else you do for the Alliance. I will have to let you go for now."

"Th-thank you, sir." Deacon nodded, "I will think about what you've told me." He was sure it would be all he thought about for the foreseeable future.

"Very good." The king hung up.

Deacon stared at his phone.

"Did you chat on the phone while climbing the tree and taking those shots?"

He turned to see Walker standing there grinning at him. He motioned to the crowd that had gathered, "they filled us in."

Giana came over the railing, her gaze moving over his chest. "You're bleeding."

Deacon looked down to see the scratches and scrapes. He wiped his hand over his skin, noting that most had stopped oozing blood. "I didn't know I was climbing a tree when I gave you my shirt." He looked at Walker, "did you see any cause for the bear to be acting that way?" He dropped down to one knee and closed the rifle case. "I hate killing an animal unnecessarily."

Walker nodded, then bent down to slip his shoes on. "It looked like its one leg was torn up from a trap at some point."

"Are bears common around here?" Picking up the case, he swung it over his shoulder.

"Not that far out of the bush."

Deacon turned his hat around the right way. "You might want to check on where the traps are," he scanned the group and saw there were a lot of young shifters, "you don't want a first-timer to land in one."

Walker nodded, "yeah, I'll go mention that to dad now."

Giana turned around. Her father and two brothers were walking through the crowd.

"I'll run interference while you go get a shirt," Walker tapped the side of his neck, reminding Deacon that with no shirt Giana's mark was very visible.

"I'll go grab you a shirt." Giana hopped over the rail and ran for the van.

Deacon watched her brother get in his father's way, likely telling him about the traps.

Oren turned to his other sons and motioned in the other direction.

Deacon was pretty they'd just been sent to go run the land and search for traps.

Giana came running back and handed him one of his shirts.

He held out the rifle case to her and then pulled it over his head, jamming his hat back on afterward. His mind was still swimming from the phone call. He made fast work of tucking the shirt in when her father stepped over the rail.

Before the Alpha could reach them, a little girl came running over to the rail. A woman ran after her and stopped her from climbing it. It was the little girl from down in the gorge, he was sure of it.

Deacon acknowledged Giana's father and held up his hand as he went over to the girl. He leaned down on his knees to look at her. "Are you okay?"

She nodded and leaned against her mother's side.

Deacon stood up and looked at the older sister that had been down there with her. "Zariah?" She nodded. "You did a good job, getting high enough and out of reach." She looked at him with a frightened expression on her face and sheltering your sister.

"I was so scared," she whispered.

"Me too," he told her.

She looked at the tree, "did you really climb the tree and shoot the bear?"

Deacon looked up in the tree, "I did." As he examined it now, he wasn't sure he'd do it a second time.

"Thank you." Her mother said with emotion shaking her voice.

He felt Giana come up beside him.

The woman bowed her head, "thank you, Giana."

With a shrug, she looked up at him, "it's kind of what we do," she told her, with an understanding smile on her face.

Deacon turned to see her father patiently observing the interaction. "Excuse us." He said quietly and went over to him.

"Thank you," Oren looked down at his daughter, noting she still held his rifle case, "both of you." He turned back to Deacon, "I just had an interesting conversation with Shepard Addison," he paused when Walker came over, "concerning you Mister Parrish."

Deacon sucked in a quiet breath, wondering if the king had told him he was his daughter's mate.

"And my daughter's new role in the Alliance's system."

Giana gave Deacon a guarded look, she was expecting the worst as well.

"I'll admit, I was quite taken back by it, but I do see the need for such a thing." He held out his hand to Deacon, "if I can ever assist in your task, don't hesitate to ask." He shook Deacon's hand and then released it. Turning to his daughter, he put his hand gently on her shoulder. "Please be careful, Giana." He stepped back, "I know you have other tasks to do today, so we won't keep you any longer." He walked back toward the crowd.

"I'm sorry, did I miss some sort of miraculous event in the last half hour?" Walker smirked as he buttoned up his shirt.

Giana shook her head and looked at Walker, the confusion was clear on her face. "I have no idea what happened." She glanced back to Deacon, then gave her brother and shrug, "Maybe the king told him what we've already accomplished with the team?"

Deacon knew exactly what the king had told her father, but there was no way he could explain it right now—not when he hadn't thought it through and had an idea of what it meant. He rubbed his hand over his beard, "I say we get going before he changes his mind."

Giana's eyes went wide. "Yes." She nodded. "Yes, let's get out of here before the magic or whatever that was wears off." She grinned at Walker and then gave him a quick hug.

"Be safe, babes." He told her softly. She nodded and lifted the rifle case to her shoulder.

"Love you, bro." She stepped over the rail and went toward the van.

Walker smirked at Deacon, "you will explain to her what happened, right?"

Deacon couldn't mask his surprise.

Glancing at his father, Walker shrugged, "I heard him telling Mom."

Blowing out a breath, Deacon nodded his head slowly, "yeah, as soon as I figure out what the hell just happened, I will."

Holding out his hand to him, Walker grinned, "you just became my father's equal—*that's* what happened."

Deacon shook his head and took his hand.

"Try to keep her out of trouble." Releasing his hand, he walked away.

Deacon looked over to see Giana sitting in the driver's seat. "I'll try." He said to no one and stepped over the rail.

Chapter Twenty-Eight

Deacon stared out the window as Giana drove. She'd been pushing the speed limit since they left her clan an hour ago. He was trying and failing at not thinking of what the king had told him. There was no way he was suddenly an Alpha in the Alliance. He dragged his hand over his beard for probably the tenth time in a span of a few minutes. He didn't doubt the king had the power to do that, if he said it was fact, then it was. Deacon Parrish an Alpha? He started to reach for his beard again, then dropped his hand and looked at it. The child of clan less rouges that spent most of his childhood getting in fights and barely surviving, an Alpha? There had to be some catch. There was always a catch. Some sort of condition that wasn't spoken, but still existed and you only found out after it was too late.

Deacon's animal was anxious, and he had only himself to blame. The constant merry-go-round of his thoughts right now was enough to drive anyone crazy. He needed to distract himself and get out of his head. Usually going for a run helped with that, but as he was stuck in the van, that wasn't an option. He glanced over at her again, she looked as tense as he felt. Both hands gripped the steering wheel like it was a battle of strength. "You can probably slow down now. You left all of your demons behind about twenty minutes ago."

He watched her grin, but she didn't look at him. "You never know." She glanced at him, humor in her eyes, "if my father had a change of heart, he'd have no problem sending his hounds of hell for me."

Deacon stared at her for a moment, "you call your brothers hounds of hell?"

She nodded, "yes, well, three of them." She eased off the gas, "Walker goes against them almost as much as I do."

"I like him."

"He's pretty likable."

Deacon took off his hat and set it on the dash, "did your father send him down to the gorge?"

Shaking her head, she leaned back relaxing more, "no, Dad would have been calling someone and Walker didn't feel like waiting around."

"He could get a job with one of the teams if he wanted, he's got good reflex actions."

"Walker?" She held his look for a second, then looked back at the road, "he likes his administration job," she shrugged, "it keeps Dad off his back while he still appears to be part of the clan and Alpha family."

"So you're the only rebel." He crossed his arms and looked out the windshield for a moment. "I didn't know things were bad enough that you moved out."

She was quiet for a moment, "Dad tried to give me an ultimatum to persuade me to drop being on the co-ord team." Putting the window down, she paused and breathed the air coming in like she was suffocating as she thought of it. "It didn't work. I packed my stuff and left, just before we were to meet up with the others."

"Where do you live now?"

Giana gave him a serious look, then smirked, "you're riding in it."

He leaned and looked back in the back of the van, then back to her. "You're going to live in the van?"

"I didn't have time to think of an alternative and then I got the call that I was going across the border to be part of the other team." She gave him a quick glance, "Amari practically lives in her transport, the rest of the team too."

Deacon sat back again, "yeah, we spend a lot of time on the road too."

"I just want to get back down there and get more of ours out." She nodded, still looking at the road, "the feeling I had when those people came out, it felt like I was finally doing something worthwhile."

"The adrenalin is addictive." He watched her as she navigated a corner, "but worth it when you see them realize that they're finally free."

"I can't imagine what that's like for them, to live like that."

Deacon had seen a lot more rescued than she had, the last ones were much better off than some of them found. He didn't want to crush her feelings and tell her about those that had been in such bad condition they'd never live a normal life. His phone ringing had him stiffen. Pulling it out of his pocket, he answered it quickly. "Hello."

"Deacon, it's Jesse, we have more information."

"Hang on, I'll put you on speaker." He tapped the screen and then held the phone in his other hand so Giana could hear too.

"Where are you on your list?"

"We have one more clan to visit and then we're picking up Konner."

"You're making good time." There were voices in the background. "We're getting ready now to head down and get the safe house set up."

Deacon nodded, Illias' teammate must have found them somewhere no one knew about.

"Tomas has been busy since we were there, they've been moving a lot of their captives around, so we're going to be avoiding working in Chicago for now."

"Do you know where they're moving those people?" Giana asked, giving the phone a quick glance.

"We've been following them, yes." He chuckled, "the flyer clan members on the teams have been going for some long flights."

Deacon frowned, "how long?"

"A few states worth," Jesse said sounding amused. "Thanks to Illias' team we're able to track them and be there when they land."

He exchanged a quick look with Giana, she was as appreciative of the tech team's ingenuity as he was. "That's good."

"Listen, the first one, it's going to be messy." He said in a hushed voice. "We just got confirmation that some of those being held are from my mate's clan, they've been held for over a decade."

The emotion on Gia's face made his chest ache.

"What's the plan?" Deacon didn't want to dwell on the anticipation of the state of them too long, it would distract focus.

"We'll send out the location soon. Before you cross, you return the van and pick up a new one. Illias will be calling you with those details. Each team is picking up various items along the way, we don't want any deliveries dropped at the safe house."

Deacon watched Giana's expression go back to determination.

"Once you cross the border, check-in with Illias and he'll have the information of which safe house you're going to." He said something quietly to someone in the background. "We're setting up two, with two full teams."

They looked at each other for a moment, the seriousness evident to both. It was a smart move, using two teams to hit two locations at once, not giving Tomas time to prepare in between.

"You can fill Konner in once you pick him up. He's going to be riding with Asher."

"Will do."

"And," Jesse's tone changed, "we think part of the reason

they tracked us was because of the choppers, so pickup has been adjusted to other means."

Giana's brows creased.

"It's going to mean longer drives, so stock up on anything you'll need before you get here and don't do it all in one place," Jesse sounded tense, "and take turns going in to get them."

Deacon rolled his shoulders. "Got it."

"Who is driving right now?"

"I am," Gia answered quickly.

"Okay, I'll get Illias to send information to Deacon's phone. His team has been working hard to set up more numbers that are secure, so there's a shortlist each team will get for contacts."

Deacon leaned down and picked up his pack to get the notebook out of it.

"We're also going to need check-ins, every two hours. We can track phones, but unless you miss a check-in, we don't want to do that. It's harder to keep something like that untraceable if it's running for a long time—or something like that."

He glanced at the time, "starting now?"

"Yes. Illias will send the information of how shortly." He paused, "Any questions?"

He watched Giana shake her head. "We're good."

"Okay, we'll see you, I'd say early tomorrow morning at the pace you're going now."

"Okay, Jesse." Giana's tone had that note of back to business to it.

The line went quiet.

Neither of them spoke for a few moments. Then Giana pushed her hat back and looked at him. "It's getting serious."

He didn't want to tell her it was always serious. "It's good, bringing in another team, we can clear more places that way."

"Yeah, just as long as I don't have to work with Nox, it will be fine."

Chapter Twenty-Nine

Gia glanced at him again, he was still looking out the window. He hadn't said much since Jesse had called. The numbers and instructions came in and he put them in their phones and told her the area they were going to and hadn't really moved since.

They'd been to the last clan and given the Alpha the number and now they were on route to pick up one of his teammates, Konner. When she'd asked what he was like, he'd said he was all right to work with. That told her nothing.

If he didn't talk soon, she was going to have to turn on the radio and sing. She talked more to herself driving alone than they were now. Had it been meeting her family? They were a bit much to take in all at once. The bear had been a great way to call a halt to the talk with her parents. When the King had called, she was relieved because she knew her mother was going to share that Deacon had her mark on his neck. It didn't matter what her father said to her, she just wanted him to keep Deacon out of it. She looked over at him again, he hadn't moved an inch, still. "What's up, Deacon, the silence is killing me."

He glanced over, the expression in his eyes looked far away. Focusing on her slowly, he gave his head a slight shake, "just thinking."

"Yeah, I caught that part." She smirked, "about the operation?"

He shook his head, "no, there's no sense in thinking that to death when we don't even have any details yet." He offered a lopsided grin, "I'll think that to death after we get there, and they lay out the plans."

"Okay, so—" she waved her hand in a circle, "care to share? Sometimes saying it out loud gives it less power." Walker had used that line on her a lot when she was younger and brooding after arguments with the rest of the family.

"The king called me," he took off his hat and ran his hair through his hair, pulling it to the back of his head before jamming it back on his head, "after I took down the bear."

"That's who you were talking to?" She cringed inside, first her father and then Deacon. *Why?* "Is everything all right?" Had it been about her? She would turn this van around and go back and tear her father apart with unkind words if it was.

"I don't even know," he leaned his elbow against the window and rested his head on it, looking at her, "I can't even think it through enough to explain it."

"Share, maybe talking it out will help." She glanced at the sign they passed, "being stuck in your head isn't good with what we're heading to do."

"Yeah," he looked down to where his phone sat like it had the answers, "Calum knew about it, but they decided not to tell me when I was younger," he rubbed his hand over his beard, "I understand why," he lifted his head from his hand and tapped his temple, "I had enough going on up here when I first started training."

"To be on the incursion team?"

"To be a useful member of our society," he smirked briefly, "that's what Calum used to say."

Gia's animal was still, listening, feeling the anxiety coming from him. "There must have been a memo about that," she grinned at him, "my father uses that line a lot."

He grinned, "that's not surprising." He blew out a breath, "apparently, according to the king my mother's clan was or is rare." He pointed to his chest, "I'm rare."

He didn't sound like he believed what he was saying. "I knew that, well, Walker said something about it, but with no computer use and not being able to call anyone, he couldn't get details."

He looked at her for a moment, "I didn't know that."

She gave him an apologetic look, "I was waiting for more details before I said anything."

Deacon nodded his head slowly, "I appreciate that." He glanced out the window, "anyway if more of my mother's clan turn up, he wants me to lead a clan."

She looked at him quickly and then slowed for the next turn; she didn't say anything until she navigated around the corner. "Like be an Alpha?" Was that possible? Could the king just make anyone an Alpha? She'd only ever known of family lines being handed that task.

"Yeah," he sat forward, "what I don't get is I'm not just my mother's clan, I'm a mix..."

She gave him a bored look, "I've seen you, there isn't much fox anything in there, if there was you'd have much shorter legs and fluffier tail."

A look of amusement crossed his face, "small blessings there, I don't think I'm a fluffy tail type."

Gia grinned, "I like my fluffy tail." She sobered, knowing this wasn't the time for jokes, he was really struggling with it. "Wait, does that mean," she pointed at him, "once you quit avoiding me, of course, and put your mark on me—we'll be Alpha's of our own clan?"

Deacon gave her a puzzled look, "do two make a clan? Chances of others turning up are slim."

"We could trace your mother's line and see if more came over here." She squinted at the sign, trying to remember the route he'd laid out, "how long did your group stay off the radar, there could be a lot more out there."

His brows creased and he looked out the windshield, "it's the next right." The hat was off again and this time he put it on his knee, a focused look on his face. Whatever he was thinking about it wasn't the best memory.

Turning her attention back to the road, she thought about it. What if none ever turned up, he'd still have the respect of the community, and to her, that was more important. The way Nox had treated him was abhorrent and she was sure that wasn't the first time someone referred to his status. She looked over at him again, "I'm in." She announced in the silence of the moment.

The look on his face was shock and confusion at the same time.

Gia smirked, "I've already accepted you, Deacon, before my teeth were sunk into your neck," she motioned to his neck, knowing the mark was there whether it was hidden by his shirt or not, "in case you forgot."

"I haven't forgotten." He told her in a soft tone.

"This is a bonus for me, really, it means I get to be with my mate, with no judging." She held his look for a second before turning her eyes back to the road, "*and* I'm out from under my father's control." She raised her eyebrows and smirked, "and that is huge, as you probably know now." Gia considered pulling over to continue, but they had a lot of ground to cover, and she didn't want to arrive late. "Plus no one, not even Nox or all the other Nox types out there can look down at you again. He will automatically have to be more respectful of you." She faked an evil grin, "and me."

Deacon waved his hand like he was brushing something out of the way, "aside from this insane Alpha shit, you really don't mind having me for a mate? I'm a mixed..."

"Correction," she said loudly, "you are about ninety percent *rare* maned wolf."

"With no family."

"We don't know that yet." Gia gripped the wheel tighter and took off her hat, so she could be sure he saw her words in her eyes, "and you'll have me until we find more."

"Find? We're going to look for more?"

She nodded, "they could be out there, as lost and alone as you were."

"Gia, all I can offer you is a one-room cabin. I don't have anything else."

"I don't need anything else, and we can build onto the cabin a bit at a time." She sent him a serious look, "and we're adding indoor plumbing."

"I thought..."

She held up a hand, "just think about it, if I have to run outside in the middle of winter, I'll be climbing back in bed with icicle feet."

"That could be a problem." He cleared his throat.

"I think so." She smiled.

"Okay, indoor plumbing, but I don't have land for a clan, or the funds."

"The Alliance will help, trust me on that." Brushing the hair out of her face, she looked over to see his brow was still furrowed, "smaller homes could be built at the bottom of that winding path that leads to the cabin, that's your land, right?"

He blinked like he was stuck somewhere else, "yeah, all along there to the river."

She shrugged, "a few homes could be built there, with the cabin still somewhat private."

"I suppose." His tone told her he was getting stuck in his head figuring out the details again.

"Hey, I thought you were big on having a little faith." She held his look for a second, "everything doesn't have to be figured out today." She could feel the tension coming off him and tried to think of how to help him.

"You really don't have a problem with who I was, what I am..."

"None at all." She answered before he could think of more negative things, "I think you're an amazing man and you don't get off on telling me what to do. That's *very* important."

Deacon snorted, "I don't want to end up like the bat."

Gia grinned, "he had it coming, he scared me half to death and touched my hair."

"I need to process all this." The serious tone had returned, "to survive out there, you always had to be thinking ten steps ahead."

"I understand that." At least she was starting to. She had no concept of what it was like to live out there without a place to call home. She glanced at the dash of the van or hadn't until recently. "Just, talk it through if you need to, I'm a good listener."

Deacon reached over and touched her arm gently and then dropped his hand away. "I will."

The phone ringing startled both of them. Deacon picked it up and answered it. "Hello." His look relaxed a little. Tapping the screen, he held it out. "Putting you on speaker, Konner."

"I just got about ten messages with numbers and shit. I guess the games are on now."

Deacon smirked, "it is. We got some out and took down a bunch that was helping before we had to take a forced break."

"I'm glad they got that all sorted out. Radio silence isn't good for the mind." He chuckled.

Gia watched him grin again.

"No, it is not."

"This checking in, that's new." Konner's voice was soft but serious.

"It's needed. How much did Wynter tell you?"

"Not much, she said you guys would fill in the blanks, which brings me to why I'm calling," he paused for a second, "when will you be here?"

Gia looked around and quickly went over the route in her head, by her calculations they were only fifteen minutes out.

"At least an hour." Deacon said.

She turned and gave him a blank look, an hour? Had she misunderstood the route?

"There's something we have to do before we get there." She looked again to see him giving her a heated look and her body and fox immediately responded. She felt her cheek flush and had to jerk her head back to keep an eye on the road.

"Perfect. I'm going for a swim, absorbing as much water as I can. This lake was a dead end, but the water is clean and who knows if we'll be anywhere near a decent lake or have time for it once we're on the job."

"How many days can you go now?"

"Three before I start to turn into flakey fishman." Konner didn't sound amused when he said it.

Gia stared at the road. *Flakey fishman?*

"Three days, that's good." Deacon sounded surprised.

"Doesn't mean I'm a happy guy the whole time."

Deacon pointed to a road and snapped his fingers telling her to take it.

She sent him a confused look but slowed and turned. Maybe he knew a different route.

"Okay an hour," Konner confirmed, "I'll expect you and your partner..."

"My mate and I." Deacon said with conviction.

Gia gave him a startled look and had to force her attention back to the road. It wasn't paved and looked like it was rarely used.

"That's new," Konner said slowly. "I look forward to meeting the brave soul that took you on in about an hour."

"See you then." Deacon hung up the phone.

Chapter Thirty

Deacon pointed to the treed area up ahead, "just pull in there." His heart was beating too fast, the back of his neck felt hot, and his animal was just as much a mess as he was. Everything hit him all at once. He had a mate and she accepted him the way he was. No one did that, not even *he* did that. Deacon realized he'd be an idiot to think for a moment more that he could be beside her and not claim her. She wanted to find his family if any remained. He wasn't even sure he wanted to find out, but if he did, having her beside him? Then he could take any outcome.

With a concerned look on her face, she pulled over under the tree and put the van in park.

"We have to talk." He opened the door and couldn't get out of the vehicle fast enough. His boot got caught on the door frame and he came close to landing on his face. Stumbling clear of the van, he went and stood under the tree.

Staring at the dead grass in front of his feet, he tried to single out one thought of too many in his head. What did he know about leading a clan? Sure, he could lead a team of armed men into serious situations or follow, it didn't matter, he was trained for either—but a clan? A clan meant women and children—how did you do that?

He shook his head, needing to back that thought up, women and children—hell, he could end up being the last of his kind. That was a sobering thought. When did he even start to care about that?

He spun around to see Gia had turned off the van and was coming around the front of it. In her hands were their run packs and phones. He'd forgotten he told her to always, *always* keep them within reach.

It felt like sweat was pouring off his brow now. It stung his eyes. The world felt like it was closing in on him, which was completely stupid, he was standing outside.

"Deacon?"

Jerking his head up, he looked at her.

"Are you all right?" She put her hand on her chest, "my fox is going crazy right now." She glanced around them, "did you see something?"

Great job. You freaked her out by acting like a moron. Shaking his head, he wiped his now damp hair back from his face. "No." He raised his hand toward her, "I'm just," he dropped it again, "having a," he shook his head again, not even knowing what he was doing, "moment," he spat out, annoyed with himself.

"Well, as *moments* go, I'm an expert on them." She gave him a soft look, "you said we have to talk."

He gave her a blank look. He had said that. "I don't," he sucked in a breath and blew it out, trying to settle his breathing, "I don't know the first thing about leading a clan." His heart continued to pound in his chest as he watched her sling the two packs over her shoulder and tuck the phones into the pocket of her jacket. She came toward him, her gaze searching his face. He felt light-headed, was it because his heart was going crazy, or had he forgotten to eat?

When she was close enough, she placed one hand on the center of his chest. "It's a good thing you have me then. I know a few things about the order of things inside a clan," she rubbed her hand against his chest and his animal stilled, "I know the inner workings of being an Alpha too." She smirked up at him, "and how *not* to do some things." Pulling his shirt out of his pants, she stretched it up and wiped his face and forehead gently. When she lowered it, her expression was serious, but understanding. "Still this little," she glanced around, "moment isn't a bad thing, Deacon."

He was having trouble focusing on her words, her voice was soothing, and touch calmed him, but her scent filled his every pore, and his mind became even harder to collect his thoughts. His animal was settled now, Deacon could have happily stood there all day, just like this. It felt like his heart was beating normally now too.

He frowned when he realized she was watching him more carefully. "It's not?" Somehow his brain had rewound what she'd said so he could speak.

"No," she gave her head a little shake, "it's not. It's a big responsibility and the fact that it's affecting you like this means you're not taking it lightly and that's a good thing."

Deacon would just have to take her word for it. Sucking in a breath, he placed his hand over hers where it now rested under his shirt. "I don't know the first thing about being a mate, or part of a family—or clan. What if I'm not good at it?"

Gia held his look, no judgment in her eyes. "There are no rules or guidelines to being a family, Deacon, that's something you figure out as you go." The heat of her palm against his chest helped him to focus and keep his thoughts under control. "As for the clan rules, there are some that are universal for all clans, the rest are established accordingly." She gave him a smile, one that made him feel like he could do anything. "And you'll have me to help keep you in line there."

He looked down at her, his heart felt like it was going to swell right out of his chest. He liked her this close, where he could see the gold flecks in her eyes and the dusting of freckles across her nose. Someday he wanted to just look at her and memorize the pattern they made. Now was not that time, they were supposed to be heading back to work. He was supposed to be more together than he was right now too.

Putting his hand against the side of her neck, her hair weaving between his fingers, he looked down at her, "you're going to have to keep me on task. I don't know anything about any of this."

"We'll take it a bit at a time." Her tone was soothing, "figure it out together, I'm sure it will all fall into place."

"That sounds a lot like have a little faith." He felt like he could draw breath again with her right here.

She smirked, "it's a pretty good line."

Deacon's mouth twitched, "it's not a line." He cradled her face between both hands, "it's a mantra of sorts, when shit starts going crazy, sometimes all you need is to have a little faith that you'll get through it."

"It seems to work." Her eyes were filled with the light of humor.

He nodded his head slowly, "it does." Leaning down, he brushed a soft kiss over her lips, tasting her. He didn't think there would ever be a day he wouldn't need to. For five years he'd done nothing but think about her right in front of him, like this. Resting his forehead against hers, he breathed in her scent, "are you sure you want a mate like me?"

"Hmm, let me think." Her voice was breathless, "yes."

"Okay, there's just one condition." He lifted his head so her could see her face completely. With stone-cold seriousness, she looked up at him. "No ax if you're upset with me."

Gia grinned, then she rolled her eyes, "fine, no ax."

"Good. Because you honestly scared the hell out of me when I saw that poor decapitated bat." He couldn't hide his smile.

"I have a condition too."

"Name it." He'd dig up a mountain and relocate it if she needed him to.

"I want a family, but not until we free more of our people. I need to help with that."

Deacon brushed the hair back from her face, "well, I have about five years of fantasies to fulfill, so we'll see how things stand in five years?"

She blushed, "okay." She licked her lips, "five years of fantasies?"

He nodded his head slowly, brushing the hair back from her neck, "yeah, and uh," he leaned down and kissed where he planned to put his mark on her, "right now I feel like I should get the award for bad timing."

"Why is that?"

When she leaned into him, his animal went crazy, she was close, and he was taking too long to claim her as theirs. "Because we have to get Konner and get across the border." He kissed her mouth softly, "I wasted a lot of time at the cabin avoiding you."

"I noticed." She ran both hands up under his shirt now. "I do have my home on wheels," she looked at the van, "right there."

"Your home," he said in a low tone, "is the cabin."

Gia looked back up at him, defiance in her eyes and he thought for sure she was going to have more objections. "My *home* is wherever you are." Lifting her chin, she reached up and tugged his beard, so he had no choice but to bend down closer, "now claim me as yours, Deacon." She moved her head to the side.

"I don't know if I can stop with just that." He brushed his mouth over the soft skin on her neck and moved it along the path, tasting it.

"I don't think you'll hear complaints if you don't stop." She placed her hand on the back of his neck.

Deacon's animal was still but poised, waiting. The wanting to be had gone on long enough, the need to have her as their own. His heart was pounding, adrenalin running fast through his body. The taste in his mouth was more his animal than it was his own. Running his tongue across his teeth, he felt the sharp edges, with a low growl, from deep in his chest, he bit into her soft flesh without further warning. If his animal could roar it would have right now. Holding her close, he molded her against his hard form and opened his mouth, licking across it, he hissed out a breath, even her blood tasted different.

Gia looked up at him with heavy eyes, her chest rose and fell. "I think we have a little bit of time; Konner didn't sound ready when we spoke to him."

Deacon leaned down and ran his tongue over her lips, "he did sound busy." Bending his knees, he wrapped his arms around her and boosted her up on his body. She attacked his mouth as he started to walk, and it was all he could do to remember how to move his legs to take steps.

When they reached the van, he braced her against the side of it to open the door. It took two tries to find the coordination to manage it. He would never get enough of her taste. Kneeling inside the door, he went to move his other leg when both phones went off in her pocket.

Stopping, he lifted his head and watched her fumble to get one of them out of their pocket.

"Message," she panted, "drive faster, we have a new window of opportunity coming up." She continued to look at the phone.

Deacon blew out a breath and took the phone from her hand. "It went to every phone."

"It's important." She stated in a breathless voice.

"Yeah." He was saying every cuss word he could think of inside his head when she rubbed her hands on his chest.

"Then we go, get Konner, now." She knelt in front of him, her hands trailing down his arms. She smiled at him slowly, "we'll get a room together now at the safe house," she tilted her chin to the side, "now that we're mated."

Grasping her hips, he moved her further away from him, "the safe house is roughly, four hours from here."

"Four hours?"

He nodded and he stepped out of the van, "plus we still have to stop and get our lists, so five hours—possibly six."

Gia lifted her chin, "I'm driving." Reaching over, she closed the van door right in front of his face.

Deacon grinned as he opened the passenger door. "Should I call Konner and tell him to wear a helmet?" Getting in, he closed the door and made fast work of putting his seatbelt on.

Gia started the van and then turned and looked at him, "maybe."

Spirit

Animal Senses Series Book 7

By Jacqueline Paige

Chapter One

Konner stepped outside and inhaled slowly. The air was cool and damp, he'd take that over the dry air in the house. The planning part always got on his nerves. He understood the need for it, but once he left the safety of the Sanctuary, he liked the action. Idling, and just biding time never sat well with him. One of the main reasons he was part of the incursion team was for the action. Too much of his daily routine was standing around waiting—and running things. He liked that once he was called out for the team he wasn't in charge, didn't have to run anything or figure out the plan—the possibility of violence was a nice bonus as well, he had a lot of frustration to burn off.

Glancing back at the house, that three mated couples were in, he blew out a slow breath and walked over and sat down on the steps of the gazebo. That was going to be uncomfortable, being around all the side-looks and secret smiles. At least they weren't here long enough that he'd have to walk around in there with his breath held so he wasn't breathing in the staunch odor of sex. He didn't begrudge them to find their mates, he wasn't that much of an asshole. Repopulating his almost extinct clan was heartbreaking and it left him a little jaded too often.

Thirteen. There were thirteen of his people left. *So far*, he reminded himself like a mother would a child. He wasn't giving up until he'd searched every single body of water on the planet.

Popping open the buttons on his shirt, he pulled the material apart so the shirt he wore underneath was exposed to the damp air. Looking down at it, he rubbed his hand over it and was satisfied to feel it wasn't dried out. Thousands of dollars had been spent to design this piece of material that was the exact opposite of a wetsuit. Instead of repelling moisture, it soaked it up like a sponge. It wouldn't sustain him by any means, but it did delay the need for finding water.

He'd watched carefully when Deacon had driven them to this location, hoping to catch sight of a lake or even a pond that would suffice if needed. The operations started at dusk tonight, two of them back-to-back, so with a little luck, he wouldn't need to go for a swim before they were back on the road heading to the next step in bringing an end to Aiden Tomas' empire.

He tracked his new partner, Asher, as he came out of the house and went to where he'd parked the van under the tree in the backyard. He'd never worked with him personally, but a few of the others on his team had and all accounts retold said he was a silent, focused man. Konner could relate to that and be thankful there would be no awkward cordial conversations with him.

Opening the pocket on his pants, he pulled out his phone, the one that was not part of the Alliance's gear. Tapping the screen, he checked for messages and was happy there were only two. The first one was from his great aunt, Alviva, the Alpha of his clan, he smirked wondering who she'd gotten to type it for her. Modern technology was not something she got on well with. She had a feeling that this was going to be a good trip for him, and she looked forward to meeting who he would bring home with him. Rubbing his hand across his forehead, a little harder than necessary, he closed it without a reply. He wasn't going to call her 'intuition' bad, but it had been nine years since he'd found one of theirs and he was a little more skeptical than she was.

The second message was from Auburn, reporting that two of the construction contracts were fulfilled and he had two more for Konner to approve before he sat down and roughed out plans for them. He read the names and didn't recognize them, but he'd do his checking when he had a few moments. Turning off the screen he leaned on his knees, at least their construction business was thriving. Clans from all over North America were building. Konner's clan didn't need the money, not really, they had more than they could ever spend.

The ache in his chest started, the one he got when he thought about the thousands of his kind that were gone. At one point there had been so many of them, they'd split up across the map into smaller groups to live near small lakes so they could stay off the radar of one-forms. There wasn't a day that went by that he didn't regret his predecessor's decision to do that. That had been their downfall. Without modern communication, help hadn't been easily gotten when they were hunted.

Ten years ago, he'd visited the last location and collected up the hidden records and clan accounts and taken them home to add to the others. He used the accumulated money of the lost to look after the remaining members and search the globe for more.

The sound of a door had him look up. Calum Dante was walking toward him. He'd never met the man personally, but he knew his reputation. He smirked, during Alliance council meetings, his name was mentioned more than the word 'funding', so his being here on these operations, almost insured the success of the objectives. He was a big man and there was no question in Konner's mind that he was a cat predator in his other form, the way he moved was silent sure and he was aware of every nuance around him.

He sat straighter as he reached him. Calum's inquisitive look landed on the phone he held. Konner smiled slow, "it's secure and approved." He motioned to the house, "one of the tech team members, Fallan, set it up for me last year, to keep in touch with my Alpha and business dealings." He left out the part where the searches on his computers at home would alert him to any possible headlines in the news he should know about.

Calum leaned against the side of the gazebo and nodded his head. "Construction, isn't it?"

"Mainly," Konner didn't feel the need to share that he had his hands in many profitable pies. Many of which helped the Alliance as well as his clan's portfolio.

Calum rubbed his hand along the back of his neck. "I have a few jobs to add to your list."

"Oh?" Konner was good with discussing business. It kept his mind off other things he didn't need weighing him down right before the operation.

"You probably already have the one for Blair's clan. The Eldon-Sorum clan."

Konner lifted the phone, "I just read that we have a work order for them."

Calum motioned to the house, "that's Blair and Kobie."

"They're expanding?" This would save him researching the clan if they were right here.

"Long story short, Tomas got all but nine of her clan, we recovered several from him on the last run. Blair became Alpha when he mated Kobie, so he's young and freaking out," Calum grinned, "and he needs more housing."

"Wait, Blair, he's the one that took out his own brother..."

"That's him."

"Wynter gave me the rundown. Nox explained it in *great* detail to her, which," he smirked, "thrilled her, to say the least." Konner nodded, "I'll let Auburn know to get on the plans for that right away." He meant it too, his own kind were scarce, but any clan that had found their lost loved ones and brought them home deserved top priority in his mind. "What's the other one?"

"The other one is a little more complicated." Calum looked amused.

"Complicated how?" Konner tucked the phone back into the pocket and gave Calum his undivided attention.

"Well, Deacon," he motioned to the house again, "has just become an Alpha of a newly registered clan under the Alliance."

Deacon was an Alpha now? Konner tried to remember what he was in his other form but couldn't recall ever seeing him shift. "I'm a little surprised we have so many new Alpha's on this operation, shouldn't they be at home looking after things?"

"Blair and Kobie are meant to do this." He motioned around them, "Deacon, he has no others in his clan as of yet."

Konner's chest tightened; he knew the pains of that all too well. "What happened to them?" He liked Deacon, they worked well together. They hadn't mentioned a thing about any of this on the drive.

"We don't know yet. Gia wants to search and has no real idea where to start," Calum gave him a calculated look, "his kind originate from South America."

Now he had his attention. "South America?"

Calum nodded, "I talked to Shep to get the ball rolling with communications," he looked down at him, "but as you know it's a shitshow right now with everything else going on." He cleared his throat, "we don't know who to trust down there now and who not to." He rolled his neck, in the first sign of tension since he started talking, "Ambassadors are on the suspect list until proven otherwise." He gave him a pointed look, "maybe you could share contacts with Gia."

Konner sucked in a quick breath, he knew Calum had more knowledge than probably the Alliance, but he was certain his business was kept between a few only. He also hadn't been informed about how serious things were within the Alliance.

Calum gave him a steady look, "everyone that comes in contact with Devin Addison I know about." His tone was quiet. "You are not the exception."

"They were supposed to be here."

"Yes. Took a lot of loud words to get Devin and Rayne to

stay away this time, but after the last one blew up, I wasn't taking chances."

Konner nodded; thankful he didn't have to worry about VIPs right now on top of everything else. He didn't want to share things about his life with a stranger, but if there were other lost clans out there, it would be wrong to not help point them in the right direction. After all, he'd found all the ways not to search. "I can talk to my contacts down there and get them to check around. What clan are we looking for?"

"Maned wolf. We need to know how many came here and if any remain there."

"Maned wolf." Konner blew out a steady breath, "I might have to look that one up."

Calum grinned, "I believe Deacon had to as well."

Konner smiled, "and I thought I was lost at times."

"Deacon was the epitome of lost once upon a time, but now," Calum looked over and watched his mate as she was talking to Kobie outside the door, "with Gia, he's on the right path."

"What's the clan name?"

"Parrish." Calum looked back at him, "I doubt there are any orders for them, but I know his mate wants indoor plumbing and at least one other building put up, just in case others are found."

Konner couldn't help but grin, "I'll get on that indoor plumbing right away."

"She would cherish you if you did."

Calum straightened from where he leaned as his mate started toward him. "I apologize in advance."

Konner looked around, "for?"

"My lovely mate is going to grill you on information about your kind, for medical reasons."

"I've heard she's an apt healer." Konner didn't know why she'd need information on his though, he wasn't intending on getting injured.

Calum chuckled, "apt doesn't describe the speed she absorbs information and data." He held out his hand as she reached them.

"Robbie is doing so much better." Shaelan smiled up at him, "he may be able to try a shift later this week."

Calum lifted their hands and kissed hers, "for which you'll want to be present."

She smiled up at him, "of course."

Shaelan was a lovely woman, peace seemed to ooze from her every pore. Konner had been on the team that was called to her clan to clean up the—*insane* shit that had been happening. He'd heard the stories and still didn't see this woman in front of him taking down the corrupt false Alpha.

He stood up, needing to feel respectful toward her. "How is your mother doing?"

She gave him a surprised look, "she is less frantic now." She smiled, "the clan is doing great though, seems tv and microwaves made everyone happy."

He couldn't help the smile that formed, "modern technology is a wonder."

"It is." She lifted the tablet in her hand. "A whole library in the palm of my hand." Her smile was big.

Calum sighed, then motioned to the steps Konner had been sitting on, "you might as well get comfortable, she no doubt has endless questions."

Shaelan gave the side-eyed look, "I need to know things in advance to be the most helpful."

"I know." Calum kissed her hand again and released it.

Konner elected to stand for the time being. "I'll try to help."

"The Alliance doesn't have a great deal on your kind, it's Konner, right?" She looked down at the tablet then back to him.

He nodded. "There's a good reason why they don't, by the time they started collecting health information and data on my clan, there wasn't many of us left."

The compassion on her face was clear as day. "I know. I'm sorry."

He could feel the emotion coming from her and it was genuine. He only inclined his head, not wanting to get into that part regarding his clan.

"I just need to know how to better help, so next time when we..."

Konner jerked his head to look at her, "next time?"

"Oh," she looked to her mate, "I thought you knew."

Calum swore softly, "shit has been so out of sorts since they breached the system." He swore again, "I thought Devin had contacted you."

Konner did sit down now before his legs gave out beneath him. They'd found one of his clan? "Where?" He looked from her to Calum.

"The last house we breached before we had to go off the grid for a week."

"She was in very poor health." Shaelan said quietly, "Deacon found her lying in the bathtub..."

Konner looked down at his hands until he could mask his emotions. *She*. They'd found a female.

"Every bone in her body was basically visible, I-I..."

The emotions pouring off her had him snap out of his grief, he looked back up at her. "Bathwater, city water, wouldn't have sustained her." He told her quietly.

"I started an IV drip, trying to rehydrate her, but I'm afraid it didn't do much."

Konner blew out a breath, trying to steady his emotions before he spoke. "A regular saline solution is a mere band-aid, a temporary fix."

Shaelan nodded, the emotion no longer on her face, now she had a clinical expression and one that said she needed more information. "Is there something I need to have on hand to help immediately?" She held the tablet up, her hand hovering.

"The saline, if no freshwater source is close at hand will stall further deterioration, eating a protein bar and other snacks the teams carry won't do much." Reaching into the pocket of his shirt, he pulled out one of the packets he always carried and held it out to her.

She took it and flipped it over, reading the ingredients.

"It's dehydrated kelp and seaweed," he lifted his hand

toward it, "and other plants that have the properties we require." He watched her tuck it into the hand that held the tablet and start typing onto it. "Mixing it with distilled water will restore some strength."

Shaelan nodded, "how much can they have at once?"

"As many as needed, it's our form of a protein bar." He shrugged a shoulder, "my clan drinks it as you would water on a daily basis."

She nodded again and kept typing, then paused and looked at the packet again. "Where do I get this?"

Konner held out his hand for the tablet, "may I?"

"Oh, yes," she handed it to him, he looked down at it and didn't bother to read the information she'd typed, he knew the number by heart and typed it onto her screen before holding the tablet out to her again, "call there, tell them it's for Konner Flores and they will ship whatever you need without question."

Shaelan glanced at her mate, and then turned, "oh," she stopped, "cuts, abrasions?" She made a face, "and young ones, are they treated the same?"

"Distilled water poured over it—it needs to be distilled so it's chemical-free, or lake water if it's handy, same for our eyes," he glanced at Calum, "if they're dry." He pointed to the package she clutched in her hand, "a paste with that if it's bad." He was happy she wanted the information but knew the chances of coming across any of his own for her to need it were next to never, especially children. "Our young ones are no different than any other child," he shrugged, "they're able to swim when they're born, but don't go through the change until they're around ten." He motioned to his eye, "the only way to tell is the silver ring around their pupil, it expands underwater to absorb reflections beneath the surface." When she leaned closer, he lowered his head so she could see his eyes. "Was there anything else you needed to know?"

"No. Thank you. I need to call Rayne, we need distilled water," she looked at the packet and started walking, "a case of this Biotrien, all teams need it on hand..." she kept walking, talking to herself.

Calum watched her for a moment and then turned and looked down at him, "she's on a mission now." He cleared his throat. "I'm sorry you weren't informed. Shit went sideways fast." He motioned to his mate that stood outside the door with the phone against her ear now, "Shae went in the chopper to Devin's campground with her…"

Konner inhaled through his nose slowly, "I understand." He did, mostly. "I wasn't reachable for a few days, so it's no one's fault." It still would have been nice to see her, maybe go and make sure her body was put to rest in the way of his people. On the floor of the water to feed the environment so new life could grow. He couldn't think about that now. "Where are they in finding out how the Alliance system was breached?"

"They're weeding through the trail slowly, I'm told." He paused as Konner stood up, "You were out looking when you picked up to come here."

It wasn't a question. He couldn't hide the surprise on his face.

Calum shrugged, "I noticed the coordinates weren't anywhere near your very fortified sanctuary."

If Konner learned something with certainty today it was that all the hype about this man in front of him was well earned and correct. "I was. I track news headlines and any oddities near water, I go search it."

Calum nodded, "I'll keep that in mind and give you a heads up if I hear of anything."

"I appreciate that."

"How many have you found?"

Konner eyed him for a moment, having help from a man like Calum Dante could never be a bad thing. "Not as many as I hope for. The last one was nine years ago, and two years before that."

Calum held his look, no emotion on his face at all. Without further talk, he nodded, "here's hoping we find more on these operations." He glanced at the house, "I'm going to see if they sorted out the lack of a flyer on team two."

Konner watched him walk away. He touched the phone through the material, debating for a moment if he should inform his Auntie that one had been found and lost. Sighing, he gave his head a shake. He'd do that in person after he was back home.

He was almost to the house when Deacon came out the back door, his fiery little mate right on his heels. He still couldn't believe he'd found a mate and become an Alpha since the last time they'd been out together.

Deacon stopped and spun around to look at her. "What the hell do I know about meetings and," he waved a hand around rapidly, "councils?"

Konner smirked, seeing Deacon seated at one of the dry council meetings was more than a little entertaining. He didn't relish them, himself, but his aged-set-in-her-ways great aunt refused to go. She outright refused to leave the Sanctuary in the past five years.

"I can help with that." Giana Marin stepped right up to him and rubbed her hand over his chest.

Konner could see the tension settling in the big man immediately. He sighed and walked toward them before his heart started aching from the demonstration of what a mate's union could bring to a chaotic world. "Sorry to intrude," he offered a polite grin, "I overheard." He motioned to where he'd been walking, "I *may* be able to help."

Deacon gave him a quick look, "you have a way out of this council *stuff?*"

Konner smirked, "not necessarily." He stopped a respectable distance from the man's mate. "I go to them for my Alpha, she doesn't care for the modern society much."

Gia smiled up at her man, "see," she held out her hand toward Konner, "he can give me the run down and I'll represent for us."

Deacon blew out a breath, reaching and clasping his hand over hers still where it rested on his chest. "I don't do politics." He said in a gruff tone.

"I know." She smiled at him, "I *know* how it works though and we need the Alliance to help us find your family and others like you."

Konner paused to wonder what this little mate was if she wasn't the same kind as Deacon. Shaking his head, he got back to the task at hand. "Calum and I were just discussing my contacts in South America," both turned to him, their focused gaze zeroing in on him like he was to be dinner, "I have no problems getting them to check around for you while they're doing the same for me."

Gia smiled at him, "that would be awesome. Thank you."

Konner inclined his head, noting that Deacon didn't seem nearly as enthused as his mate, in fact, he looked a little green like he might want to throw up. "It's no problem, I understand the pains that go with searching for surviving members."

Her expression changed to compassion, "I'm sorry to hear that, but thank you for helping us."

He nodded, then cleared his throat, he couldn't deal with much more female compassion today. "I was also told you want indoor plumbing and another building erected?"

Deacon nodded now. "The indoor plumbing ASAP before the ground freezes I guess."

"I'll get that started." He paused as he reached for the phone in his pocket, "oh, it's my clan construction company that," he motioned to the house, "is why Calum was talking to me about it."

Gia bobbed her head, "that's handy, that you're here with us."

He inclined his head; no words were necessary. "It might be a week before I can get someone there, but I'll get Auburn to contact you for details." He pulled the phone out, "what sort of building are you wanting?"

"Oh," Gia looked up at Deacon for a moment, "I think a small functional two-bedroom for now?" She watched her mate as she spoke, "just in case." She smiled up at him, then turned to Konner, "I think it would be a little too cozy to share the no bedroom cabin."

Deacon rolled his shoulders, and turned to look at him, "I have ideas for the cabin too," he pointed to the house, "maybe after we do this, we can talk about it."

Konner nodded, "I'll just put some of Auburn's time on hold then and get the details to him later."

"We'll have to talk about financing…"

Konner shook his head as he typed a message to his clanmate, telling him to expedite Blairs and more rushed things were on the way. "Don't worry about the financing right now, the Alliance is helping with clan expansions since we've had to rearrange our lives for safety purposes." Sending the message, he looked back up at them, "We'll worry about all the finer details at a later date but getting the plumbing in before winter is a *now* thing." He offered a polite smile.

"Yes." Gia gave him a big grin. "Definitely a *now* thing."

"Guys."

They all turned to see Jesse standing at the door.

"I guess we better get back." Gia took Deacon's hand. "Thank you, Konner."

Deacon gave him an appreciative look before following her back.

Konner looked over to see his riding partner coming back from the van. He hadn't lied, entirely about the Alliance funding, he just left out the part that it was his foundation that initiated it.

"Ready to kick some ass?" Asher asked him as he walked by. "I am more than ready."

Konner put the phone away and followed the tall lanky shifter into the house. He could only hope there were asses to be kicked at this point, he needed to burn off the anger of another lost member of the water clan.

About Jacqueline Paige

I am a multi-published author of 'all things paranormal'. My book list proves this is my niche with my stories of witches, ghosts, psychics, shifters, and more now on the shelves. My current genres are paranormal romance, paranormal fantasy, and paranormal romantic suspense.

My books are available in many formats around the globe, including book/reading apps. Since adding them during the pandemic, my books have had over a million reads and my 'to be written' list is growing longer each day. I can't write fast enough.

I began my writing career in 2006 (as a joke) and my first book was published in 2009. I haven't stopped since then. I am an avid reader and will read 'anything with words', whether it's a novel, article, or even every sign I pass.

I live in Ontario, Canada in a small town that's part of the popular Georgian Triangle area. Even though I can see the mountains, I do not ski.

When I'm not in one of my writing worlds, I spend time with my grand-monsters.   I have nine of them (so far) and I look forward to corrupting them in the years to come.
Jacqueline also writes under the pseudonym of J. Risk

Jacqueline loves to hear from her readers, you can find her at

http://jacquelinepaige.com/

Author note:

Did you enjoy reading one of my books?

If so, PLEASE help spread the word on social media. You can help by sharing on Facebook, tweet about it, post something on Instagram, Pinterest. Posting a review on your favorite book sites go a long way to help authors. With your help in keeping my books "out there", I can continue writing to keep those stories coming.

Writing and promoting can be very time consuming. I love talking to readers, but the hours spent on keeping so many social media outlets current can become overwhelming and time for writing pays the price. If you can take a few minutes to help, that would be awesome. Thank you!

9 781990 763137